A Recipe For Love

B. Oneirova

To my mother,
Who showed me that love flows through the simple act of cooking,
As her hands created magic in our kitchen,
And who taught me to cherish beautiful stories
As I watched her lose herself in the pages of her books.
Your passion lives on in every word I write.

And to my readers,
May this story be a warm embrace for your heart,
A gentle respite from life's worries,
And a reminder that sometimes the most unexpected ingredients
Create the most delicious recipe for love.

In cooking and in love, the most powerful transformations happens over slow heat, with patience, and the courage to try flavours that have never before been combined.
The secret to any extraordinary creation - whether on a plate or in life lies in finding that perfect balance.
- Bianca Almeida

Contents

Foreword

Dear Reader,

There's something magical about the way certain stories come to life—much like the perfect dish that seems to create itself when the right ingredients meet at the right moment. "A Recipe For Love" began as a dream and then a simple idea: What happens when a talented chef and a homesick athlete cross paths? But as I wrote, it transformed into something far richer and more complex.

This novel explores the intersection of passion and profession, of ambition and belonging. In Bianca and Pablo, I wanted to create characters who are masters of their crafts yet still searching for something more—that indefinable flavour that makes life complete.

When I first imagined Bianca standing in her kitchen in Rio, I could smell the garlic and onion frying in the pan and feel the warmth of Brazilian sunshine streaming through her window. Similarly, when Pablo stepped onto that London field for the first time, I felt both his exhilaration and his profound loneliness. These characters arrived in my imagination fully formed, carrying their hopes, dreams, and hungers.

Food and love share a beautiful symmetry. Both require patience, attention to detail, and a willingness to take risks.

Both nourish us in ways that transcend the physical. And both, when done right, create memories that sustain us through our darkest moments.

In writing this story, I've drawn from my own experiences with cultural displacement, the power of shared meals, and the unexpected ways love can transform our carefully laid plans. While Bianca and Pablo's journey is uniquely their own, the emotions they navigate—homesickness, professional pressure, and the vulnerable act of opening one's heart—are universal.

As you turn these pages, I hope you'll find yourself transported—to the vibrant streets of Rio, to the hushed excitement of London, to the intimate space of a kitchen where two people discover that the ingredient they've been missing might just be each other.

Thank you for joining Bianca and Pablo on their journey. May their story remind you that sometimes the most extraordinary recipes are the ones we never planned to create.

With warmth and gratitude,

B. Oneirova

Prologue

They say that the fastest way to someone's heart is through their stomach. But hearts are complicated things, aren't they? They hunger for more than just sustenance. They crave connection, understanding, the familiar taste of home when you're far from everything you know.

In Rio de Janeiro, food was never just food. It was conversation and celebration, comfort and tradition—layers of flavour that told stories of past generations. The sizzle of garlic and onions hitting hot oil, the rich aroma of beans simmering with bay leaves, the vibrant colours of fresh produce against weathered cutting boards. These were the rhythms of life, as natural as breathing.

But when you leave home, when oceans separate you from everything familiar, those rhythms change. Food becomes fuel. Meals become routine. The soul of cooking —that indefinable magic that transforms ingredients into memories—fades like a photograph left too long in the sun.

For some, this fading is bearable, just another sacrifice made for ambition and dreams.

For others, it creates a hunger that no protein shake or nutritionist-approved meal can satisfy.

It's a particular kind of homesickness that settles in the

stomach first before working its way to the heart.

Sometimes, the cure for this hunger arrives in unexpected ways. Sometimes, it walks through your door with knives and recipes and the scent of vanilla clinging to dark hair.

Sometimes, fate serves up exactly what you need, in a form you never anticipated.

And sometimes, the dish that begins as comfort food becomes something else entirely: a feast for two hearts discovering they share the same hunger.

This is a story about food and football, yes. But more than that, it's about finding home in another person's arms, about the recipes we create together that no one else could possibly replicate.

Because the most powerful ingredient in any kitchen isn't found on any shelf.

It's the love we stir into every moment we share.

Chapter One: A Dream and a New Game Begins

Bianca stood at the edge of the stage, her heart pounding with excitement and pride. Golden sunlight streamed through the university hall's windows, casting a warm glow over rows of graduates in their navy blue robes. She adjusted her cap, a rush of emotions washing over her as she clutched her Nutrition diploma. At just twenty-one, she had envisioned her future many times, but nothing felt more real than this moment. Years of studying, experimenting with flavours, and learning the science behind food had led her to this day.

With dark hair cascading down her back and sun-kissed skin glowing under the tropical Brazilian sun, Bianca radiated confidence and determination. Cooking had always been her passion—more than just a skill, it was an art, a way to bring people joy. While her classmates discussed clinical positions and hospital internships, she knew she wanted something different. She wanted to bring nutritious, delicious meals to people in a way that felt personal and meaningful.

Her best friend Elena appeared at her side, beaming with pride. "We did it! Can you believe it? And I heard Antonio's parents are throwing a graduation party tonight. Please tell me you're coming."

Bianca smiled but shook her head. "I can't. I've got that meeting with the potential client I told you about —the fitness influencer who wants weekly meal prep."

Elena groaned. "You're already working? We just graduated!"

"That's the point," Bianca replied, a determined glint in her eyes. "I need to start building my business now. This could lead to more clients."

Within weeks of graduation, Bianca launched her business as a personal chef. She developed a unique service— going to clients' homes, preparing customized meals for an entire week, and leaving them carefully portioned and frozen. What started as a small venture, cooking for busy professionals and fitness enthusiasts, quickly gained attention. Her meals weren't just healthy; they were vibrant, full of flavours, and tailored to each client's needs.

Word spread quickly. One referral led to another, and soon Bianca found herself cooking for Rio de Janeiro's elite—actors, influencers, and even professional athletes. Social media played a massive role in her rise. Clients raved about her delicious meal plans, sharing photos and recommendations, turning her into a sought-after chef.

Despite the long hours and demanding nature of her job, Bianca loved every moment. Every dish she prepared carried a piece of her heart, and every satisfied client fuelled her motivation. She was building something special, a career on her own terms.

Little did she know that her culinary journey was about to take her far beyond the bustling streets of Rio —straight into an unexpected adventure that would change her life forever.

Pablo had dreamed of this moment his entire life. Standing on the grand field of his new club in England, he took in the sea of empty seats, imagining the roaring crowd that would soon fill the stadium. At just twenty-one, he had achieved what so many young Brazilian footballers aspired to—signing with one of England's elite clubs. It was an opportunity of a lifetime, but one that came with challenges he hadn't fully anticipated.

Tall and athletic, with brown skin and striking green eyes, Pablo embodied the essence of a carioca—a boy from Rio who carried the effortless charm and confidence of his hometown. He had spent years training, pushing his limits, and proving himself on the field. Football was his passion, his escape, and now, his career. But moving to England meant facing a whole new world, and not just because of the intense competition.

The weather was cold and grey, a stark contrast to the warm sun of Brazil. The language barrier made things harder, but worst of all was the food—bland, unfamiliar, and nothing like the comforting meals he had grown up with. He had tried to adapt, eating the meals prepared by the club's nutritionists, but they lacked the warmth and flavour he craved. Training on an empty stomach or forcing down meals he didn't enjoy wasn't sustainable. He needed help.

His teammate, Juan, noticed his struggle during practice. "You're looking thinner, man," he commented sympathetically as they stretched side by side. "Not enjoying the food from the club's nutritionists?"

Pablo grimaced. "I try, but it's like eating cardboard. I miss real food—rice, beans, properly seasoned meat, fresh salad."

"I went through the same thing when I first came here," Juan said, tapping him on the shoulder. "You should talk to your agent. Maybe hire someone to cook for you."

Later that evening, Pablo slumped onto his couch, his phone buzzing with a message from his agent, Leo, asking how he was feeling. The pressure of adjusting to life in England, both on and off the pitch, was beginning to weigh on him.

Pablo: *"Hey Leo, I'm struggling to get used to the food here. It's so different, and it's affecting my energy. You know how important it is for me to stay in top shape."*

Leo: *"I get it, man. It's tough when you're far from home, and I know how particular you are about your diet. Why don't you consider hiring a personal chef? I've heard other players doing it—especially those who need their meals tailored for performance. You can find someone who really gets your needs. I can help you find one if you want?"*

Pablo: *"I didn't even think about that until Juan mentioned it this morning. Do you think it would make a big difference?"*

Leo: *"Definitely. I've heard a lot of players rave about the help they've gotten. Maybe even check out a few social media pages for recommendations. You deserve to have someone who can really take care of your meals. It'll help you get back on track faster."*

Pablo: *"Okay, thanks man, that sounds like a plan. I'll look into it tonight, and if I can't find anything, I'll let you know."*

Chapter Two : The Unexpected Message

That night, scrolling through social media, Pablo came across a post that immediately caught his attention. A famous Brazilian actor had shared a glowing review about his personal chef, a young woman who prepared nutritious, customized meals. This was exactly what he needed—the right kind of food he was used to and loved, something to help him adapt and stay fit.

Without wasting any time, he clicked on the profile —@ChefBianca. As the page loaded, his eyes widened. The photos were stunning—beautifully plated meals that screamed fresh, vibrant, and packed with flavours. They looked both heartwarming and homely. Satisfied clients praised her skills in every post, and there was an offer for exclusive services, which was exactly what he was looking for.

"This is it. This is exactly what I need," Pablo thought to himself, impressed. *"Nutritious meals, but still delicious. I need someone who understands how to keep me in top form without feeling like I'm stuck eating bland, tasteless food, plus it's like all the foods I'm used to and miss from home."*

For a moment, he sat back, his thoughts racing. *"She's exactly what I've been looking for."* His fingers hovered over the screen. *"But she is all the way back in Brazil, dammit,"* he hesitated briefly before clicking "contact me" to message her.

Hi, Bianca. I saw your work online. I just moved to London for football, and I'm struggling with the food here. Forgive the unexpected message, but after weeks of bland protein shakes and nutritionist-approved meals that taste like cardboard, I found myself lost in your Instagram. Those colours, those flavours... I'm wondering if there's any possibility you might consider a temporary culinary rescue mission to London? I promise it will be worth your while.

A man of few words and straightforward by nature, Pablo couldn't help but feel a mix of excitement and nervousness after sending the message. What if she said no? What if she didn't have time? He would have to get back to his search, but for some reason, he felt a connection with her posts.

Meanwhile, it was a sunny afternoon in Brazil. Bianca was shopping for fresh produce at a market in Rio de Janeiro when her phone buzzed. It was a message from an Instagram account she didn't recognize.
Bianca frowned, hesitated, then opened it.

Pablo Costa. The Pablo Costa. Rising star of Brazilian football and just signed to one of the premier clubs for a record-breaking sum. His face was plastered across billboards throughout Rio, that camera-ready charisma selling everything from sports drinks to luxury watches. Bianca stopped for a minute and found a coffee shop to go in and sit down, needing a moment to process it all.

London, she thought.

The word alone sent a jolt of adrenaline through her system. She had dreamed of international experience—

staging in kitchens across the world, absorbing techniques and flavours beyond Brazil's borders. But those plans had always been a "someday thing."

Her finger hovered over the reply button. This was ridiculous. Probably a prank. Why would Pablo Costa reach out to her directly? And even if it was legitimate, picking up and moving to London for a temporary position was impulsive, unprofessional, and possibly career suicide.

Yet something—curiosity, ambition or both—made her type:

"Hi, Pablo! Wow, what an opportunity for you. Congratulations! Thanks for getting in touch with me. I'm not sure if I am what you're looking for, but I'd love to help. Can you share what you're looking for exactly?"

When Pablo saw her reply, he couldn't hide his excitement and responded immediately.

Pablo: *"I'm struggling with adjusting to the food here. I know it's not your typical gig to do it abroad, but I was hoping you could help me in a 3-week trial period? Help me to batch cook and freeze some healthier, home-cooked Brazilian meals while I'm here?"*

Bianca hadn't even finished reading the whole message when her phone pinged again.

Pablo: *"It could be a trial period for three weeks in London. I know it's a lot to ask, but I can cover travel and accommodation. I'd like to see if we're a good fit and if this is something you could consider."*

Bianca's heart raced as she read the messages. Could she really take this leap? London. It felt like a dream, but it was also real. Butterflies fluttered in her stomach.

Bianca's throat went dry. The offer was real!

She asked the waitress for water and a strong espresso, her mind racing. Three weeks in London. Working for one of Brazil's most famous athletes. The exposure alone could catapult her career to international recognition.

But it was also reckless. She had established clients here, a routine, security. What if it didn't work out?
What if Pablo was impossible to work with, or worse? She'd heard the rumours about footballers.

She typed carefully:

"I'm very flattered by your offer, Pablo. Thanks a lot, but I'll need to think about it. Can I get back to you soon? Also, maybe it would be good if we could video call and chat about what you need or want and then discuss some more details?"

Professional. Cautious. Ball back in his court.

His reply came almost instantly:

"That's a great idea. Just let me know when and what time. I'm off this week, so I will make it work when it is convenient for you."

Bianca stared at her phone, her carefully ordered world suddenly tilting on its axis. She should call her parents. Or Elena, her best friend since childhood. Someone who would talk sense into her.

Instead, she found herself typing "London culinary scene" into the search bar on Instagram, her pulse quickening with each keystroke.

Just research, she told herself. Just being thorough.

But deep down, something else was stirring—something that felt remarkably like the first tremors of excitement before a leap into the unknown.

Chapter Three: The First Taste

The video call was scheduled for nine the next morning —afternoon in London. Bianca spent an embarrassing amount of time deciding where to sit (kitchen, to emphasize professionalism), what to wear (crisp white button-down, hair pulled back), and how to appear (competent, not desperate; interested, not overeager).

Her laptop screen flickered, and suddenly he was there.

Pablo Costa looked different from his billboards. Less polished, more human. His dark hair was slightly rumpled, and he wore a simple grey t-shirt that stretched across broad shoulders. But it was his eyes that caught her— green, startlingly bright against his golden-brown skin, and carrying a weariness that no photoshoot had ever captured.

"Hi, Pablo! Nice to meet you," Bianca said, her voice steadier than she felt.

His face brightened with a smile that transformed him from tired athlete to the charming superstar she recognized from advertisements. "Hey, Bianca! Thanks for taking the time to chat."

His voice was deeper than she'd expected, with the distinctive rhythm of Rio's accent—a sound that immediately made her feel at home despite the ocean between them.

"I'm really glad you reached out," she said, folding her arms casually on the counter. "So, how can I help you?"

Pablo ran a hand through his hair—a nervous gesture that seemed at odds with his public persona. "I'm having some trouble adjusting to the food here in London. It's not that I don't like it, it's just... it doesn't feel like home, you know? I need something that's still nutritious for my training but with the flavours I'm used to." He paused, his expression turning slightly embarrassed. "The club has nutritionists, but everything tastes the same. Like... nothing."

Bianca nodded, understanding immediately. "Food is more than nutrition—it's comfort, it's memory, it's connection. Especially when you're far from home."

Relief flashed across his face. "Exactly. I saw your posts, and honestly, it looks like exactly what I need.
Something that meets my training requirements but actually tastes like food."

"I can definitely help with that," Bianca said, feeling a spark of professional excitement. "So, you'd want me to prepare meals for you in your place in London? You mentioned a three-week trial?"

"Yeah," Pablo nodded eagerly. "I can provide accommodation—there's an apartment a few floors below mine that I can arrange. You'd have your own space, complete privacy. I know it's asking a lot to relocate temporarily, but—" he hesitated, then added with disarming honesty, "I'm kind of desperate. Those protein shakes can only get you so far."

Bianca laughed, some of her nervousness dissolving. "I

understand completely. I could prepare meals for you several times a week, leaving things properly portioned and stored. We'd work around your training schedule, of course, and I'd need to know your specific nutritional requirements."

"That sounds perfect," Pablo said, leaning forward slightly, his eyes brightening. "Would that work for you? The three-week trial, I mean."

Bianca took a deep breath. The sensible answer was to request more time to consider, to ask for references, and to negotiate terms in writing.

Instead, she heard herself say: "Yes. Let's do it."

Pablo's expression shifted from hopeful to elated so quickly that it was almost comical. "Really? That's— that's amazing. I honestly thought you'd say no."

"I surprise myself sometimes too," Bianca admitted with a small laugh. "But this feels like a good opportunity. For both of us."

They spent the next twenty minutes ironing out details— when she would arrive, what kind of kitchen access she would have, his schedule, dietary preferences. Pablo was surprisingly thorough, asking thoughtful questions about what equipment she might need, offering to stock any ingredients ahead of time.

As the call wound down, Bianca felt her initial trepidation giving way to anticipation. This was impulsive, yes, but it also felt right. A challenge, a change of scenery, a chance to push herself beyond her comfort zone.

"I'll have Leo—my agent—contact you with the travel details tomorrow," Pablo said. "And anything else you need, just let me know."

"I will," Bianca promised. "And Pablo? Thank you for the opportunity."

His smile softened. "Thank you for saying yes. I have a feeling this is going to work out great."

After they disconnected, Bianca sat in her kitchen for a long moment, the enormity of what she had just agreed to washing over her. Three weeks in London. Working for Pablo Costa.

She needed to call Elena.

Her best friend picked up on the first ring, as if she'd been waiting for the call.

"Well?" Elena demanded without preamble. "Was it really him? What happened?"

"It was him," Bianca confirmed, still slightly dazed. "And... I'm going to London. In two days."

There was a beat of stunned silence, then Elena's squeal of excitement nearly shattered Bianca's eardrum.

"You're WHAT? Oh my God, Bia! London? With Pablo freaking Costa? Are you serious?"

Bianca laughed; her friend's enthusiasm was infectious. "Yes, I'm serious. It's just a three-week trial, but—"

"But it's LONDON! And he's gorgeous! And this could be huge for your career!" Elena rushed on, barely stopping for breath. "Tell me everything. How did he look? Was he nice? Did he flirt with you?"

"Elena! It's a professional arrangement," Bianca protested, feeling her cheeks warm. "He needs a personal chef who can cook Brazilian food. That's it."

"Mmhmm," Elena hummed, clearly unconvinced. "We'll see about that. Now start from the beginning. I want every detail."

As Bianca recounted the conversation, she found her excitement growing. Yes, this was impulsive. Yes, it was a risk. But maybe, just maybe, it was also the beginning of something extraordinary.

Pablo ended the call and sat back in his chair, a weight lifting from his shoulders for the first time in weeks. She had said yes. Somehow, this complete stranger had looked at him through a screen and decided to upend her life to come work for him.

He hadn't expected it to be this easy. Something about her directness, her obvious passion for food, her quiet confidence—it had all felt immediately right. Like finding a solution to a problem he hadn't fully articulated until that moment.

His phone buzzed with a text from Leo.

"Well? Did Chef Instagram agree to your crazy proposition?"

Pablo typed back: *"She said yes. Can you handle the arrangements? Flight, apartment rental, contract?"* Leo's reply came instantly: *"Already on it. Hopefully, you will stop being grumpy now."*

Pablo rolled his eyes, though he couldn't deny Leo had a point. With his emotions in such turmoil lately, he had been particularly irritable. He knew it, even if he didn't want to admit it out loud.

Pablo was thinking about the video call, Bianca was striking—her dark eyes intelligent and assessing, her smile transforming her serious expression into something warm and approachable. But that wasn't the point. He needed her skills, not a distraction.

He set his phone down and wandered into the kitchen, opening the refrigerator more out of habit than hunger. The same uninspiring contents greeted him. Soon, he thought with a flicker of anticipation, this space would be filled with real food again. Meals that tasted like home, that would fuel not just his body but his spirit.

For the first time since arriving in London, Pablo felt a spark of hope. Maybe, just maybe, this place could eventually feel like somewhere he belonged.

Chapter Four: First Meeting

London materialized beneath the plane in a patchwork of grey and green, so different from Rio's vibrant coastline that Bianca felt a momentary pang of doubt. What was she doing here, really? Flying across an ocean on the word of a man she'd spoken to once, to a city where she knew no one, where even the air felt foreign?

But as the plane touched down with a gentle bump, she straightened her shoulders. This was an adventure, she reminded herself. A chance to prove her abilities beyond her comfort zone. Three weeks.
She could do anything for three weeks.

The first-class experience—another surreal aspect of this whole endeavour—ended with priority deplaning. As Bianca followed the signs to immigration, she mentally rehearsed her explanation for this trip. "Private chef, temporary work arrangement, three weeks only." Simple, professional, unmemorable.

She had just cleared customs when she spotted a man in a crisp suit holding a tablet with "BIANCA ALMEIDA" displayed on the screen. Leo, Pablo's agent, she presumed. He was shorter than she expected, with carefully styled hair and a smile that was simultaneously warm and assessing.

"Bianca? Welcome to London!" His accent was pure Rio,

his handshake firm. "I'm Leo, Pablo's agent and occasional babysitter. The car's waiting outside."

The drive from the airport was a blur of new impressions —iconic landmarks she'd only seen in movies, streets teeming with people speaking a dozen different languages, architecture that spanned centuries. Leo kept up a running commentary, pointing out places of interest and peppering her with questions about her work, her background, her expectations.

"Pablo's really excited you're here," Leo said as they approached the sleek high-rise where she would be staying. "I haven't seen him this enthusiastic since he signed with the club. You've got some kind of magic touch, chef, and you haven't even cooked for him yet."

Bianca smiled politely, unsure how to respond to the subtle insinuation in Leo's tone. "I'm just doing my job. He misses food from home—that's something I understand completely."

Leo studied her for a moment, then nodded with what looked like approval. "Good answer. Pablo needs people around him who see him as a person, not a paycheck or a tabloid headline." His expression grew more serious. "He's having a tougher time adjusting than he lets on. The club, the press, the fans—they all want pieces of him, and they don't much care what that costs him."

Bianca nodded, absorbing this glimpse behind the public persona. "That sounds incredibly difficult."

"It is," Leo agreed. "But you know what? I think your cooking might be exactly what he needs right now. A taste of home, a bit of normalcy in the tornado his life has become." He grinned suddenly. "Plus, if you fatten him up a bit, the female fans will be devastated, which might give him some peace."

Bianca laughed and said: "I'm not sure his nutritionist would approve of that strategy."

"True," Leo conceded. "Although, between you and me, those club meals taste like cardboard with protein powder."

The car pulled up to a modern glass tower, and Leo led her through a private entrance, explaining security procedures, the amenities available, and how to access both her apartment and Pablo's. As the elevator ascended, Bianca's nerves returned. Would she be cooking for him immediately? Should she have prepared something in advance, or at least researched ingredients?

But when the elevator doors opened on her floor, Pablo was nowhere to be seen. Instead, Leo showed her to a stunning apartment he had rented for her with floor-to-ceiling windows that framed London's skyline in dramatic relief.

"Pablo wanted to give you a day to settle in," Leo explained, handing her a key card. "He's got team meetings until evening anyway. You can cook tonight's dinner here at your place then from tomorrow you can start at his place. You'll find the kitchen fully stocked based on the list you sent—he insisted on handling that personally. Anything else you need, just call me." He handed her a business card. "Pablo said he'd come by around seven, if that works for you?"

Bianca nodded, relieved. "That's perfect. Gives me time to orient myself in the new kitchen."

After Leo left, Bianca explored the apartment, which was easily twice the size of her place in Rio. The kitchen was a chef's dream—state-of-the-art appliances, pristine countertops, and every tool she could possibly need. Opening the refrigerator, she found it meticulously stocked with everything she had requested, plus a few additional items—Brazilian coffee, pão de queijo mix, her favourite brand of chocolate that wasn't exported to the UK.

The thoughtfulness of these details surprised her. Either Pablo was extraordinarily considerate, or he was desperate for a taste of home. Perhaps both.

She unpacked quickly, then spent the afternoon exploring the building—it had a gym, a pool, a small cinema, and several other amenities that spoke to the exclusive nature of the people that lived there. By six, she was back in the kitchen, familiarizing herself with the layout, planning the evening's meal.

She decided on feijoada—Brazil's comfort food at its finest and complex enough to showcase her skills. It would take time to develop those flavours, but she suspected Pablo would appreciate the effort. She had just begun preparing the ingredients when the doorbell rang.

Her heart quickened, and she wiped her hands on a towel before answering.

Pablo Costa stood in the hallway, looking both more and less like his photographs than he had on the video call. Taller in person, his athleticism evident in the breadth of his shoulders and the lean strength of his frame. He wore simple jeans and a white t-shirt, his hair still damp as if he'd just showered.

But it was the expression on his face that caught her off guard—a mixture of anticipation and genuine nervousness, so at odds with the confident superstar image she'd expected.

"Hi," he said, his voice warmer and deeper than it had sounded over the video call. "You're here."

Bianca smiled, extending her hand. "I am. It's good to meet you in person, Pablo."

Instead of shaking her hand, he leaned in for the traditional Brazilian greeting—three alternating kisses on the cheeks. The familiar gesture in this foreign place made her chest tighten with an unexpected wave of homesickness.

"Sorry," he said, catching her surprise. "Force of habit. Welcome to London."

"No, it's nice," she admitted, stepping back to let him in. "A little piece of home."

He followed her inside, his eyes taking in the kitchen where she had already begun working. "You've started cooking already? You didn't have to do that tonight—I know you just got here, and jet lag is brutal."

"I'm fine," she assured him. "And cooking helps me settle in new places. I thought feijoada would be a good first meal— unless you'd prefer something else?"

Pablo's face lit up with such genuine delight that Bianca couldn't help but laugh. "Feijoada? Are you kidding? That's perfect. I haven't had a proper one since I left Rio." He moved closer to the stove, inhaling deeply. "It already smells like home."

Something in his voice—a vulnerable note beneath the enthusiasm—touched her. "That's the idea," she said softly. "Food is more than nutrition. It's memory, comfort, belonging."

He looked at her with an expression she couldn't quite decipher—surprise, perhaps, or recognition.

"Exactly. The club nutritionists... they don't get that. It's all protein counts and recovery formulas to them."

"Well, I promise this will meet your nutritional needs, but it'll taste like actual food," Bianca said, returning to the counter where she'd been organizing ingredients. "You got everything I asked for, and then some."

Pablo grinned, looking slightly embarrassed. "Yeah, I might have gone overboard. But I wanted to make sure you had everything you might need."

"The chocolate was a nice touch," she said, raising an eyebrow.

"I have excellent intel," he admitted. "Your Instagram has several posts about that specific brand." "You did your research," she noted, impressed despite herself.

"When it comes to food? Always."

There was an easy rhythm to their conversation as Bianca continued preparing the meal. Pablo leaned against the counter, asking questions about her cooking techniques and sharing stories about his favourite meals in Brazil, his eyes following her movements with undisguised appreciation.

"Usually, I won't eat with my clients," Bianca found herself saying as she plated the food.

Pablo raised an eyebrow. "Am I that intimidating?"

She laughed. "No. I just like to keep things professional, plus I would be cooking at your place."

"Ah." He looked momentarily disappointed. "Well, this is a special case, isn't it? First night, new job, new country. Plus, my agent said we should get to know each other a bit since we'll be working closely."

Bianca hesitated, then nodded. "I suppose one dinner wouldn't hurt."

They sat at the kitchen island, and Bianca watched with unmistakable satisfaction as Pablo took his first bite. His eyes closed briefly, and a low sound of pleasure escaped him.

"This..." he opened his eyes, looking at her with genuine awe. "This is incredible. I feel like I've been transported back home."

Pride bloomed in her chest. "I'm glad it tastes like home."

"Better than home," he admitted. "My mother would be jealous—don't tell her I said that."

As they ate, the conversation flowed easily. Pablo was surprisingly down-to-earth, asking thoughtful questions about her career, sharing candid stories about his adjustment to life in London. There was none of the arrogance she might have expected from someone of his fame and status.

The smile that broke across his face was worth the impulsive decision. "That's...that's really great. I can't tell you how much I've missed food like this. Real food. Food with soul."

"Everyone deserves to eat well," she said simply. "Even famous footballers."

Pablo laughed, the sound warm and genuine. "Especially famous footballers. We're very delicate creatures, you know. Fragile egos and all that."

"I'll keep that in mind," Bianca promised, smiling as she cleared their plates.

As he was leaving, Pablo paused at the door. "Thank you, Bianca. Not just for the meal, but for coming all this way. I know it was a lot to ask."

The sincerity in his voice warmed her more than she expected. "It was an easy decision, actually.
Sometimes you have to step outside your comfort zone to grow."

He nodded, holding her gaze for a moment longer than necessary. "Well, I'm glad you stepped into mine. I have a feeling these are going to be a good three weeks."

After he left, Bianca cleaned the kitchen with methodical precision, trying to make sense of the evening. Pablo Costa was nothing like she had anticipated—more vulnerable, more genuine, more... human. It would be easy, she realized with a sudden jolt of clarity, to forget that this was just a job. To start seeing him as something more than a client.

That, she decided firmly as she turned off the lights, was a complication she could not afford. Three weeks. Professional boundaries. Then back to Rio and her real life.

Simple.

So why did it already feel anything but?

Chapter Five: A Different Kind of Chemistry

The first week unfolded in a surprising pattern of comfortable routine. Bianca prepared meals around Pablo's training schedule, crafting nutritious breakfasts, recovery lunches, and dinners that balanced the club's requirements with the flavours of home. Pablo's gratitude was evident not just in his words but in the way he savored each bite, often closing his eyes as if to fully absorb the experience.

"This is heaven," he declared after trying her moqueca, a rich Brazilian seafood stew that she had adapted to fit his nutritional plan. "How did you get it to taste this good while still keeping it lean?"

Bianca smiled, pleased by his reaction. "It's all about building flavours in layers. You don't need excessive oil or cream if you know how to coax the natural flavours from the ingredients."

For the next three weeks, she dedicated herself to the job. Twice a week, she arrived at Pablo's home, filling his kitchen with the rich aromas of home-cooked Brazilian meals. She prepared feijão tropeiro, grilled chicken with quinoa, rice and beans, salads, hearty stews, and balanced post-training meals, all carefully stored and labelled.

Pablo was barely home, traveling for games, but he sent her messages after every meal.

"This is amazing. You have no idea how much I missed food like this."

"Can we add more protein next week?"

"You are a lifesaver."

Bianca smiled every time she read Pablo's messages. Though they barely saw each other in person, their exchanges over text felt meaningful and full of promise. It was strange how they'd managed to form a connection despite the physical distance between them, but the little conversations they had brightened her days. The best part? The pay was incredible. What she earned from Pablo in two days was more than she made in Brazil in an entire week.

On the days when she wasn't cooking for him, Bianca threw herself into exploring London. She was determined to make the most of this new chapter in her life. As soon as she finished her work and had some free time, she would head out, her eyes wide with curiosity and excitement at everything this city had to offer.

One morning, Bianca woke up early and decided to check out the Borough Market, just a short walk from where she lived. The vibrant food stalls greeted her with an explosion of colours—fresh fruits, artisan cheeses, homemade breads, and an array of spices that filled the air with their intoxicating aromas. Bianca wandered from stall to stall, sampling everything she could: tangy goat cheese, warm cinnamon rolls, and the most flavourful roasted nuts she'd ever tasted.

"This is a paradise," she muttered to herself as she tucked

a small jar of honey into her bag. The market was bustling with locals and tourists alike, each person animated by the food, the energy, and the unique culinary offerings. Bianca couldn't get enough.

Later that afternoon, she ventured to a hidden gem she had discovered online—a quaint little café known for its innovative fusion of British and Asian flavours. Bianca sat at a corner table, savouring every bite of her miso-glazed fish and sipping on a cup of rich green tea. She smiled, realizing that her world had expanded so much in just a few short weeks.

Sometimes, she would meet up with other chefs she had met on social media or through friends of friends, learning new techniques and hearing about their experiences. Bianca loved to exchange ideas, and she quickly realized that in London, the culinary world was buzzing with creative minds. She felt more alive than ever, surrounded by such diverse cultures and flavours, all contributing to her ever-growing passion for food.

One day, she decided to take a class on traditional French pastry techniques, something she'd always wanted to try but never had the chance to in Brazil. The kitchen was filled with laughter and chatter as they all kneaded dough and filled delicate pastries with rich creams. Bianca's hands moved with ease, the flour dusting her fingers as she learned the intricate art of making perfect éclairs.

As the class came to an end, the instructor walked over to her with a warm smile. "You've got a natural touch, Bianca. You should definitely try this more often."

Bianca beamed with pride, her love for cooking and learning growing every day.

Bianca also found herself exploring the lesser-known parts of London. She visited local food trucks offering everything from smoky barbecued meats to fragrant curry dishes. She enjoyed wandering through neighbourhoods like Camden, where eclectic cafés and street food stalls lined the streets. Each corner seemed to hold a new adventure for her— another taste, another experience. It was thrilling to be part of this new city, with its endless culinary possibilities.

At night, as she curled up in her flat, Bianca would go over her notes from the day, mentally cataloguing everything she had learned. She would make lists of dishes she wanted to recreate, new ingredients to try, and ideas for new meals she could offer to Pablo. She thought about how much she was growing in her craft, and how much more there was to discover.

Bianca couldn't help but feel grateful for the opportunities she was having in London—working with Pablo was just the beginning. There was so much more out there waiting for her. She loved the way her life had unfolded, and while she knew there were challenges ahead, she was determined to embrace them all. Her passion for cooking, the exciting food scenes, and the new connections she was forming— everything was coming together. And she was only just getting started.

The weeks had flown by, and just like that, the trial period was over. It was a Saturday night, and they had agreed to meet at Pablo's place to discuss what came next. Bianca felt a mixture of excitement and nerves as she arrived, but the moment she sat down, Pablo wasted no time.

"I want you to stay," he said simply, leaning forward with an earnest expression. "Your food has been a game-changer for me. If you're willing, I'd like to offer you a full-time contract for a year."

Bianca's heart pounded. A year in London? Traveling, learning English, and building her business internationally? She had already thought about this possibility, but hearing it out loud made it real.

Without hesitation, she beamed. "Yes! I'd love that."

Pablo grinned, clearly relieved. "Seriously? That's amazing." He ran a hand through his hair, looking genuinely excited. "I was worried you'd say no."

Bianca chuckled. "Are you kidding? This is an incredible opportunity. I mean, I love working with you, and London has been a dream."

Pablo let out a breath, sitting back in his chair. "That makes me so happy to hear. My agent has already drafted the paperwork. We'll sort everything properly—salary, bonuses, travel expenses, all of it. I want to make sure this is a win-win for you too."

Bianca nodded, feeling a rush of gratitude. "That's really thoughtful. I trust you and your team, but I'd love to go through the details together."

"Of course," Pablo said. "We'll go over everything. And don't worry, I'll make sure you have everything you need. If you want more flexibility or even some time to work on your own projects, we can figure it out."

Bianca's chest warmed at his words. He wasn't just hiring her—he genuinely cared about her growth.

"I appreciate that so much," she said. "And honestly, I can't wait to experiment with even better meals for you. Now that I know your taste, I have so many ideas."

Pablo laughed. "As long as feijoada stays on the menu, I'm in."

She rolled her eyes playfully. "It's a deal. But you'll also have to trust me to push you to try new things."

"I trust you completely," he said, his voice softer now. "You're the best decision I've made since I got here."

Their eyes met for a beat longer than usual before Bianca cleared her throat. "Alright, let's make this official. Where's the paperwork?"

Pablo smirked and grabbed his phone. "I'll text my agent right now. But first..." He stood up and walked over to the kitchen. "This calls for a celebration. Wine?"

Bianca grinned. "Only if you let me pick the snacks."

"Deal."

As they clinked glasses, Bianca felt something shift. She had arrived in London with no idea what the future held, and now, here she was—securing a career-changing contract and building something she never expected.

And this was just the beginning.

Chapter Six: New Horizons

With her contract signed, Bianca was living her dream. London had become her playground—every street, every market, every restaurant was an adventure waiting to be explored. She made new friends, indulged in culinary experiences she had only ever read about, and even took spontaneous weekend trips across Europe. From savouring fresh pasta in Rome to strolling through the charming streets of Paris, she embraced every moment.

Meanwhile, Pablo's career was at its peak. He was one of the most sought-after players of the season, his name dominating headlines, his performances breaking records. Brands wanted him, clubs envied him, and fans adored him. He had everything he had ever worked for.

Yet, despite the whirlwind of success, there was one thing he looked forward to the most—Bianca's presence in his home.

Their paths, for now, remained strictly professional. She was his chef; he was her client. They exchanged friendly banter in the kitchen, shared meals from time to time, but that was it.

Or at least, that was what they told themselves.

Because something was changing.

Pablo found himself lingering in the kitchen more often,

watching her cook, memorizing the way she moved, the way she smiled when she tasted something perfect. And Bianca—despite her insistence that this was just a job—couldn't ignore the way her heart fluttered whenever he complimented her food or when his gaze lingered just a second too long.

They were walking a fine line.

And soon, something would tip the balance.

Chapter Seven: An Unexpected Shift

Pablo's world flipped upside down in a heartbeat. One wrong step, one mistimed tackle, and suddenly he was on the ground, clutching his leg, pain shooting through him like fire. The stadium went silent. He knew. Even before the medics rushed over, even before the MRI confirmed it—a torn ligament. Six months, minimum, off the pitch.

At first, he was numb. Then came the frustration, the restlessness, the sheer helplessness of watching from the sidelines while his teammates carried on without him. The days felt longer, the nights even worse. He hated being stuck at home with nothing but his thoughts and rehab sessions.

With his schedule completely turned around, he realized he'd be eating at home every day. So, he decided to text Bianca.

Pablo: *Hey, since I'm stuck here now, think you can come in more often? Maybe four days instead of two?*

Bianca: *Of course! Again, I'm so sorry you are going through this. If I can help in any way, please let me know. And the 4 days cooking works better for meal planning.*

He smiled at her message. She had a way of making things feel lighter, even when everything else felt heavy. Maybe this injury wouldn't be *all* bad, he thought, at least he would have amazing meals to eat.

The next day, as Bianca unpacked her ingredients in the kitchen, Pablo lingered nearby, watching her with curiosity. Usually, he'd just sit at the counter, scrolling through his phone or chatting with her about random things while she cooked. But today, he seemed different— more focused, more *interested*.

"Hey," he said, leaning against the counter. "Would you mind if I actually, you know... watched properly?

I've always wanted to learn how to cook well."

Bianca raised an eyebrow, a playful smile tugging at her lips. "*You*? Learn to cook?"

Pablo put a hand on his chest, mock-offended. "Wow, no faith in me at all?"

She laughed, shaking her head as she grabbed a knife and started chopping. "Fine, fine. You can watch. Cooking's more fun with company anyway."

And just like that, a new routine formed. Each time she came over, he pulled up a stool closer to the counter, asking questions about spices, techniques, and why her food always tasted *so* much better than anything he'd ever had. Their conversations started to stretch beyond just food— he'd tell her about his childhood in one of the favelas in Rio, his family, the pressures of football. She'd share stories about her childhood in Rio, the struggles of making it as a chef, her dream of one day opening her own restaurant. Then one evening, as she kneaded dough for homemade pasta, he casually threw out an idea.

"You know... I was thinking," he said, rubbing the back of his neck. "What if you actually taught me? Like, properly?"

Bianca looked up; hands covered in flour. "You mean like cooking lessons?"

"Yeah. I mean, I know you're busy, so I'd pay you, of course," he added quickly.

She wiped her hands on a towel and studied him. "You're serious?"

He shrugged. "Dead serious. I'm home all the time now, so I might as well learn something useful."

Bianca hesitated for only a second. More money meant more savings for her dream flat and restaurant back in Brazil. Plus, it could actually be fun.

"Alright," she agreed, smirking. "But if you burn your own kitchen, I *will* fire you as a student." He grinned. "Deal."

What neither of them realized was that somewhere between the spices, the laughter, and the quiet moments of just *being*, something between them had already started to shift.

Chapter Eight: Crossing Lines

Pablo's presence in the kitchen had become routine. At first, he would do simple things like stirring sauces, kneading dough, and even attempting to grill steak under her careful instruction.

"You're actually not bad at this," Bianca teased one evening, nudging him playfully as he flipped a piece of salmon.

"Are you saying I might have a backup career?" Pablo grinned, his green eyes sparkling with amusement.

She laughed. "Maybe, but don't quit football just yet."

Their easy friendship deepened. Conversations extended beyond food—Pablo told her about his struggles with fame, the pressure of expectations, and how lonely it could feel. Bianca shared stories of her childhood in Rio, how her parents had worked hard to support her dreams, and how she never imagined living in London.

One evening, as Bianca packed up her things, Pablo hesitated before speaking.

"Bianca, why don't you stay for dinner tonight, like let's order a pizza or something, give you a break?"

She asked with a smile, "Stay, you are missing fast food now?" she said jokingly

"No, I mean, you've been cooking all this time for me, you

deserve a little break." He shrugged, almost shyly. "And I wouldn't mind the company."

She hesitated. Was this crossing a line? But then again, she was hungry, and eating alone at home wasn't exactly appealing.

"Okay," she said, trying to sound casual. "Takeaway pizza actually sounds good. I'm quite tired today."

They ate at the kitchen island, talking and laughing almost as if they had known each other for years. What surprised Bianca the most was how easy it was to talk to him. He was nothing like the arrogant athletes people often assumed footballers were. He was funny, down-to-earth, and had a boyish charm that made it impossible not to smile.

It became a habit. Every so often, after cooking, Pablo would convince her to stay. They would sit for hours, talking, laughing, and teasing each other.

Then, one day, he took it a step further.

"Have you been to the cinema here in London?" he asked casually as she packed up her knives.

She shook her head. "No, I haven't actually, as I've been so eager to visit food places, castles, parks..."

His eyes lit up. "Then let's go. This weekend."

She raised an eyebrow. "You? In a public cinema?"

He grinned. "I have ways of keeping things low-key."

She hesitated for a second before sighing. "Fine. But if people recognize you, I'm running away." He laughed. "Deal."

That Saturday, Pablo arrived at her flat in a hoodie and cap, looking like someone on a secret mission.

"Subtle," she teased as she walked to his car.

"Hey, I need to avoid attention." He smirked. "Unless you want to be in the tabloids tomorrow."

They watched a comedy, sharing popcorn and whispering jokes during the movie. At one point, she laughed so hard that Pablo leaned in and murmured, "I like the sound of your happiness."

She turned to look at him, her breath hitching at the way he was staring at her. For a moment, she thought he might kiss her. But instead, he just smiled and turned back to the screen.

The cinema turned into dinner outings, late-night drives, and random coffee stops. Slowly, her life in London wasn't just about food and work anymore.

One afternoon, Pablo took her to a small café tucked away on a quiet corner. "Best coffee in London," he promised, holding the door open.

The café was cozy and understated, with mismatched furniture and soft jazz playing in the background.

They found a table by the window, where they could watch people passing by on the rain-slicked streets.

"Thank you for this," Bianca said as they waited for their drinks.

Pablo shrugged, looking almost shy. "It's nice to share the city with someone who is excited to see new things they haven't seen before. Makes me appreciate it more, too."

Their coffees arrived—rich, aromatic, and served with small pastries on the side. Bianca took a sip, closing her eyes briefly to savour the complexity of the flavour.

"Good?" Pablo asked, watching her reaction closely.

"Excellent," she confirmed. "But I might be able to improve those pastries."

He laughed, the sound warm and unguarded. "I don't doubt it. You could probably improve anything."

There was a beat of silence, comfortable but charged with something neither of them was ready to name yet.

"So," Pablo said finally, breaking the moment. "Tell me something I don't know about you."

Bianca raised an eyebrow. "Like what?"

"Anything. Something not on your Instagram. Something real."

She considered the question, stirring her coffee slowly. "I almost quit cooking after my first year in culinary school."

Pablo's eyes widened. "Really? Why?"

"I failed a practical exam—beef bourguignon. I overcooked the meat, my sauce split, everything that could go wrong did." She smiled ruefully at the memory. "I was devastated. I called my parents in tears, and told them I was dropping out." "What changed your mind?"

"My father," she said, her voice softening. "He drove three hours to my apartment, let himself in, and found me packing. Without saying a word, he went to the kitchen, took out ingredients, and started cooking. The same dish I had failed."

Pablo leaned forward, completely engaged. "And?"

"And he failed too," Bianca laughed. "Miserably. The meat

was tough, the sauce was lumpy. But he served it anyway, and we ate it together. Then he said, 'Now you know two ways not to make beef bourguignon.

That's more than you knew yesterday.'"

Pablo's smile was warm, understanding. "Smart man."

"He is," Bianca agreed. "He taught me that failure isn't the end—it's part of the process. The next day, I went back to class, and I practiced that recipe until I could make it in my sleep." She looked down at her coffee. "I still make it sometimes, just to remind myself how far I've come."

When she looked up, Pablo was watching her with an expression she couldn't quite interpret—something between admiration and recognition.

"Your turn," she prompted, trying to lighten the mood. "Tell me something real about Pablo Costa."

He hesitated, his fingers tracing the rim of his cup. "I almost quit football three years ago."

Bianca blinked in surprise. "You're kidding."

"Nope." He sighed, leaning back in his chair. "I was playing for a club in São Paulo. Big team, big expectations. I wasn't starting, wasn't scoring, wasn't anything they thought they had paid for. The pressure was... intense. Fans turned on me, the media tore me apart daily." His eyes grew distant, remembering. "I told my agent I was done. I wanted to go home, do something normal." "What stopped you?"

Pablo's smile turned wry. "Leo—my agent. He showed up at my apartment at six in the morning, dragged me to an empty training field, and made me run drills until I couldn't stand. Then he sat me down and said, 'That feeling right now? The exhaustion, the pain? That's how you know you're still alive. As long as you can feel that, you haven't failed. You've just found another way not to play football.'"

Bianca's eyes widened at the parallel. "Sounds like we both had the right people at the right moments."

"We did," Pablo agreed. "And now look at us—you're a chef cooking for international clients, and I'm..." he gestured vaguely.

"A football superstar?" Bianca supplied.

He grimaced slightly. "A guy who kicks a ball for a living and somehow ended up in London, missing feijoada so badly he imported a chef."

"Lucky for me you did," Bianca said softly.

Their eyes met across the table, and something shifted in the air between them—a recognition, perhaps, of how similar they were beneath their different lives.

"We should get back," Pablo said finally, his voice slightly rougher than before. "Before someone recognizes me and this ends up in tomorrow's tabloids."

Bianca nodded, suddenly aware of how much like a date this afternoon had felt—wandering through markets, sharing coffee, exchanging personal stories. Boundaries, she reminded herself. Professional boundaries.

But as they walked back toward their building, Pablo carrying her bags of exotic spices and specialty ingredients, she couldn't help noticing how naturally they moved together, how comfortable the silence between them had become.

Dangerous, a small voice whispered.

But for the first time since arriving in London, she wasn't

entirely sure she wanted to be safe.

Chapter Nine: The Breaking Point

Bianca had always been disciplined. She had built her business from the ground up, worked tirelessly to establish herself, and never let distractions get in the way.

So why did Pablo keep getting under her skin?

It had started with small things—his lingering glances, the way he'd brush his fingers over hers when passing her a plate, the way he'd lean a little too close when watching her cook. At first, she convinced herself it was nothing. Just Pablo being naturally flirtatious.

But the tension between them was undeniable.

One evening, as Bianca was plating Pablo's dinner, he reached over to taste the sauce with a spoon she was holding. His hand covered hers, his fingers warm against her skin.

She froze.

He didn't pull away. Instead, his green eyes searched hers, his lips quivering in amusement.

"You always get this tense around me?" he murmured.

Her pulse skyrocketed. "I— No."

His smirk deepened. "Liar."

She rolled her eyes, stepping back quickly. "Eat your food,

Pablo."

He chuckled, but there was something different in the air. Something they both knew wasn't going away.

The next time she came over, something felt... different.

The kitchen smelled of sizzling garlic and rosemary, and Pablo had just wrapped up a physio session at home. He was more relaxed, his usual quiet mood replaced with a teasing glint in his eyes. As Bianca moved around the kitchen in her apron, tying her curls into a loose bun, Pablo leaned against the counter like he belonged there.

"Teach me something new," he said, arms folded.

She looked at him with mild suspicion. "Like what? Do you want to actually learn something or just get in the way?"

He smirked. "Something fun."

With a dramatic sigh, she grabbed an egg from the counter and held it up. "Alright then, chef boy. Crack this with one hand."

He took it with far too much confidence.

It exploded between his fingers, splattering across the counter and dripping off his knuckles.

Bianca burst out laughing, her hand flying to her mouth. "Oh my god, you're a disaster!"

"Excuse me!" he protested, trying to wipe the egg off with a towel. "I'm good with my feet, not my hands."

The comment was meant to be harmless, but it hung between them, sparking something unsaid. Bianca suddenly found it hard to focus, the air between them warm, charged.

Still chuckling, she turned back to the pot, stirring its contents with practiced ease. That's when she felt him move behind her—close, too close. The scent of his cologne mingled with the food and the faintest trace of mint.

He leaned in, his voice low, velvet-soft in her ear. "You always smell like vanilla."

Her heart stuttered. She turned just enough to meet his gaze. It lingered there just a second too long— enough time to cross a line.

He kissed her.

Slow. Gentle. Testing the waters. Giving her the chance to say no, but she didn't.

Her eyes fluttered shut, and instead of stepping back, she leaned into it, her hands finding the front of his shirt, pulling him closer. His grip on her waist tightened as the kiss deepened—no longer testing, but tasting.

When they finally broke apart, she stood in his arms, breathless and blinking like she was waking from a dream.

"This is dangerous," she whispered against his chest.

He ran a hand through his hair and exhaled hard. "Yeah, it is."

Bianca stepped back, reality rushing in. "We work together."

He nodded. "I know."

"This is wrong, we crossed a line here Pablo, sorry, let us pretend it didn't happen, ok?"

"Don't do that," he interrupted, his voice soft but firm. "Don't minimize it."

She hesitated. "I came here for work. To build something. I can't get distracted, and neither can you."

Pablo leaned against the counter again, quieter this time. "Then don't let it distract you. Let it inspire you; you definitely inspire me."

She narrowed her eyes. "What is this? Some sort of footballer philosophy?"

He grinned. "Something like that."

She chewed on her bottom lip. "So, what are we doing then?"

"We're not putting labels on it," he said, stepping closer. "But we're not pretending it's not happening either, I can't help myself anymore anytime I'm near you, your smell, your voice, your eyes..."

Bianca studied him, her guard slowly lowering. She didn't want to want him. But it was already too late.

After a long pause, she sighed. "Okay. But we keep this simple. We can enjoy each other's company, but no strings attached."

Pablo brushed a strand of hair from her cheek. "Simple."

But even as he kissed her again—deeper, slower this time—they both knew .... this would never stay simple.

Chapter Ten: A Heatwave of Emotions

The summer heat in London was unlike anything Bianca had expected. She had assumed England would always be cold, grey, and rainy, but this week had been nothing but sunshine and a heatwave that made the air thick and heavy.

She had come to Pablo's house that Friday afternoon for work as usual, ready to cook his meals for the week. But the kitchen felt like a furnace. Even Pablo—who had also grown up in the scorching Rio de Janeiro summers—was fanning himself with an old magazine, shirt clinging to his back.

"This is ridiculous," he groaned, finally pulling his shirt over his head and slumping onto the couch. "Why is it hotter here than in Brazil?"

Bianca laughed, trying not to stare at his bare torso as she wiped sweat from her brow with a kitchen towel. "At least in Brazil we have air conditioning pretty much everywhere. Here, it's just suffering and tea." She glanced around his luxurious apartment with mock disapproval. "And seriously, with a posh flat like yours, how is there no air conditioning?"

"The building's over a hundred years old," he explained with a sigh. "Historic preservation laws or something. The owners are putting in central air next year."

Suddenly, Pablo sat up, a mischievous glint in his green eyes. "I have an idea."

She narrowed her eyes at him, recognizing that expression by now. "That tone implies I should be worried."

He tossed the magazine aside and stood, wincing only slightly as he put weight on his healing knee.

"Come cool off in the pool with me."

Bianca blinked. "The pool? Pablo, I didn't bring a swimsuit or extra clothes. I came here to work, remember?" She gestured to the vegetables half-chopped on the cutting board.

He shrugged with a boyish grin that made him look younger than his twenty-one years. "So? You can borrow a T-shirt and some shorts. Come on, you've earned a break. It's too hot to cook anyway."

Bianca bit her lip, glancing at the stove where a pot of rice was already simmering. The idea of diving into cool water right now was extremely tempting. And all she had left to prepare were simple dishes that could wait. "Fine," she sighed theatrically, tying her hair up into a messy bun. "But just for a little bit. I still have work to finish."

Minutes later, they were out by the pool that he had on his balcony—a stunning infinity edge design that seemed to merge with the London skyline. Bianca had traded her light summer top and jeans for a pair of Pablo's athletic shorts and an oversized white T-shirt that fell to her thighs. She felt strangely vulnerable in his clothes, surrounded by his scent.

With a quick breath for courage, she jumped straight into the deep end, not giving herself time to reconsider.

The shock of cold water was exactly what she needed. She surfaced with a gasp, laughing as the heat washed away from her skin. Pablo dove in after her, making a far bigger splash. He came up grinning, slicking his dark hair back, water dripping from his broad shoulders and chest in rivulets that caught the afternoon sun.

"Better?" he asked, swimming closer to her.

"Much better," she admitted, floating onto her back and closing her eyes against the bright sky. "This might be the best idea you've ever had."

For the next hour, they splashed and played in the water like carefree kids. Bianca tried (unsuccessfully) to dunk him, which dissolved into fits of laughter when he effortlessly lifted her and tossed her back into the water. They raced across the pool, Pablo giving her a head start even though his injured knee had not healed enough for swimming. Eventually, they ended up floating lazily side by side on pool loungers, their toes trailing in the water, sipping on iced lemonade that Pablo had fetched from the refrigerator.

"You know," Pablo said lazily, tilting his head toward her with a content smile, "this might be the best day I've had in weeks."

Bianca raised an amused eyebrow. "Really? You've got the world at your feet, and sitting in a pool all day is the best day?"

He rolled onto his side to face her more fully, propping his head on his hand. The movement caused water droplets to slide down his chest, and Bianca forced herself to keep her eyes on his face. "You'd be surprised. Lately, it's been all rehab and restlessness. This... this feels normal. Like I can breathe a little."

Bianca turned to face him, too, understanding in her eyes. Despite their different worlds, they shared the experience of being young people thrust into high-pressure careers. "Yeah. I know what you mean."

Later, they made fresh fruit cocktails together. Pablo insisted on learning, so Bianca guided him—her hands over his as he muddled mint and squeezed limes into the glasses. Every time their fingers touched; she felt a little jolt shoot through her.

They sipped their drinks poolside, laughing at his overly sour creation.

"Okay, maybe I'm not a natural bartender," he said, wincing at the taste.

"Nope," she teased. "Stick to football."

By the time they realized the time, the sky was painted in soft golds and pinks despite it being nearly 9 p.m.

Bianca stretched, stifling a yawn. "I should probably go."

Pablo frowned. "Already? It's still early."

"It's late for me," she chuckled. "And I'm freezing now."

"Want to take a quick shower before going home? I know it's in the same building but you still need to walk a few sets of stairs," he asked. "The chlorine might dry out your skin."

She hesitated. "You have a point. Are you sure it's okay?"

"Of course. Use my ensuite," he said immediately. "The guest bathroom's completely empty right now— no towels or anything."

"Well... all right then. Thanks," she said with a small smile, gathering her dry clothes from where she'd left them folded on a chair.

Inside his sleek bathroom, the warm water soothed her chilled skin, but she couldn't stop thinking about how easy it had been to spend the day with him. The teasing, the laughter... It felt natural. It felt like more.

Then she realized—there was no towel.

Glancing around, panic rising, she found nothing usable apart from a tiny hand towel. She groaned, wrapped her arms around herself, and cracked the bathroom door open.

"Coast is clear," she muttered and tiptoed into his bedroom, water dripping down her arms and legs. But just as she reached the bed—

The door swung open.

Pablo walked in, a bundle of towels in his hands, looking completely distracted—until he saw her.

She froze. So did he.

Then— "AHHHH!"

Bianca yelped, grabbing the nearest pillow and clutching it to her chest. "Pablo!"

His face turned bright red as he quickly spun around. "Sorry! Sorry! I brought clean towels! I didn't know you were— I mean I didn't— I didn't see anything! Not really!"

Bianca, mortified, snatched the towel from his hand and

fled back into the bathroom, slamming the door.

Inside, she leaned against the sink, heart racing, skin burning hotter than it had in the sun.

"Oh my God," she whispered. "That did NOT just happen."

Meanwhile outside, Pablo collapsed to sit on the edge of the bed, burying his face in his hands. He could not erase the split-second image now seared into his mind— Bianca, wide-eyed and wet, her skin glistening, her dark hair plastered to her shoulders, beautiful in her shock. He groaned to himself, half in despair and half in sheer disbelief at his own bad timing.

Keep it together, man, he thought, dragging his hands down his face. *You did not just walk in on her like an idiot.*

She came out a few minutes later, her cheeks still flushed. She wouldn't look at him.

"I'm going home now," she muttered.

Pablo bit the inside of his cheek, trying not to smile. "You sure you don't want to stay longer?"

She shot him a look. "Goodnight, Pablo."

And with that, she practically ran out the door.

As it clicked shut behind her, Pablo flopped backward onto his bed, staring at the ceiling.

This arrangement they had?

Yeah... it was definitely getting more complicated.

Chapter Eleven: A Night to Remember

Bianca had woken up that morning relieved that it was her day off—after what had happened the night before, she wasn't sure she was ready to face Pablo again just yet. The mortification of him walking in on her naked was still too fresh in her mind.

But at 10 AM, her phone lit up with a message.

Pablo: *Hey, are you free tonight around 8ish? There's a new restaurant opening nearby. Super exclusive, and no photographers are allowed in, so you don't have to worry. Everyone's bringing a plus one, and since I don't have anyone and you love food… I figured I could ask you?*

Bianca's first instinct was to say no. She was still mortified about last night, and spending the evening with him at some fancy event might only make things more awkward between them.

But then he mentioned it was a highly anticipated Arabic fusion cuisine restaurant—a style she adored and had been eager to explore in London. Her inner chef's curiosity kicked in immediately. It could be a fantastic chance to try new food, meet other chefs, maybe even network a little with people who could help her career.

After a moment's deliberation (and a pep talk to herself to not be awkward), she replied:

Bianca: Hey, thanks for the invite. I would love to go. What should I wear?

Pablo smiled at his phone. He hadn't expected her to say yes so quickly.

Pablo: *It's a black-tie event. Hope that's okay?*

Bianca: *I'll be ready by 7.*

That evening, at 7 p.m. sharp, Pablo was waiting outside Bianca's flat, leaning against the wall and checking the time on his phone for what had to be the tenth time.

He adjusted the cuffs of his crisp black suit nervously. He had no idea why he felt nervous. It wasn't a date. It was just two friends attending an event. Perfectly innocent.

Then the door opened, and he forgot how to breathe for a moment.

Bianca stepped out wearing a sleek black silk dress that hugged her curves in all the right places. Delicate straps rested on her shoulders, and a tasteful slit ran up one side, revealing a glimpse of her leg when she moved. Her dark hair was swept up in a loose, elegant twist, and a few strands framed her face. In heels, she stood nearly as tall as him, the extra height only emphasizing her poise.

She was stunning. Breathtaking. Like something from a dream.

She gave him a tentative smile, then noticed him staring. "What? Is this not okay? Should I change?" She looked down at herself, suddenly self-conscious. "I knew I wouldn't know how to dress for something like this..."

Pablo reached out on impulse, gently catching her hand before she could retreat back inside. "No," he said quickly, shaking his head. "No, you're... I mean, you look, phew...I'm just... speechless. You look absolutely stunning."

She exhaled a relieved laugh. *"Phew. Good, because I don't own anything else besides jeans and chef jackets."*

He chuckled, but his chest felt tight as she smiled at him. God, she was beautiful. And the strangest part?

He realized he was nervous—actually nervous—around her for the first time since they'd met.

Get a grip, he scolded himself as they headed to the car. He was acting like this was prom night or something equally ridiculous.

At the upscale restaurant, it seemed everyone noticed Bianca. Heads turned, people whispered, and more than one person asked Pablo if "this lovely woman" was his girlfriend. Before he could even answer, Bianca would smile graciously and say:

"No, no, we're just good friends! I'm his personal chef. He was kind enough to invite me tonight so I could experience this incredible food."

But Pablo felt the stares. He felt the subtle, appraising looks other men at the dinner table were giving Bianca, the way a few of them angled to get her attention or—much to his irritation—asked for her number under the guise of "professional connections."

Something twisted uncomfortably inside him each time someone vied for her attention. Jealousy, hot and undeniable, unfamiliar to him. He had never been a jealous person with women before.

He had no right to feel it, either. She wasn't his.

And yet... he hated the thought of anyone else having her.

Later that night

As they drove back to their place, Bianca turned to him in the dim light of the car's interior.

"Thanks for inviting me. Tonight was... really great," she said sincerely. "The food was incredible. I got so many ideas."

He glanced at her, her profile illuminated by the soft glow of streetlights. "I'm glad you had fun"

As he parked the car and they were walking back to their flats, Pablo said: "Do you... want to come in for a bit? Maybe watch a movie, or I have about a million board games, stocked up on chocolate too—"

She gave him a small, amused smile. "Sure."

Inside his apartment, Bianca immediately kicked off her heels with a dramatic groan. "Finally! My feet are killing me," she sighed, collapsing onto his couch.

Pablo laughed and slipped off his suit jacket, draping it over a chair along with his tie. He disappeared briefly and returned with two glasses of wine.

As he sat down beside her and handed her a glass, he noticed her massaging one foot and wincing.

Without thinking, he gently took her ankle in his hand. "Here, let me," he offered.

She stiffened at first. "*Pablo*—"

"Relax," he murmured, pressing his thumbs into the arch of her foot in slow circles like he'd seen the team's physio do countless times. "I know a thing or two about sore muscles."

Bianca leaned her head back against the couch. "Oh my god, that feels amazing," she mumbled, her eyes fluttering shut. "And you said you weren't good with your hands—guess that was a lie."

Pablo smirked. "My hands are good for lots of things," he teased, his voice dropping slightly.

She rolled her eyes but didn't pull her foot away. "So full of yourself," she managed, though her sigh of relief betrayed how much she was enjoying the foot rub.

He just laughed and handed back her the wine. They ended up putting on a movie, though neither paid much attention to it. They were too busy talking quietly about the dinner—trading thoughts on the spiced lamb dish, gossiping about the one pompous food critic at their table, laughing at inside jokes from the night.

Somewhere along the line, the conversation gave way to a comfortable silence. Pablo realized he was still holding her legs in his lap from the foot massage, his hand resting idly on her ankle. Her dress had a high slit, and from where he sat, he could see the smooth length of her calf and thigh. He traced little patterns on her skin with his thumb, barely realizing he was doing it.

Bianca felt her heart rate picking up as his fingers absentmindedly caressed her leg. The air between them was shifting—turning warm and heavy with an undeniable tension that had been building for weeks.

She looked at him, and he was already looking at her.

Neither of them spoke.

Gently, Pablo reached out and tucked a loose strand of hair behind her ear, his fingertips lingering on her cheek.

Bianca's breath caught.

Slowly, hesitantly, she leaned toward him.

Their lips met—softly at first, testing once again. But it didn't take long for the kiss to deepen. The second the wine glass slipped from Bianca's fingers onto the couch (thankfully not spilling as it was empty), Pablo pulled her onto his lap, his hands settling at her waist as their lips moved together in perfect sync.

She tasted like wine and something sweet he couldn't quite place—maybe the hint of vanilla she always carried with her scent.

She ran her fingers through his hair, pulling him closer, deepening the kiss. The heat between them was undeniable, consuming.

"Bianca..." he murmured against her lips, his voice rough with desire.

She didn't answer with words. Instead, she took his hand and stood, gently tugging him up with her.

Then, wordlessly, she led him toward his bedroom.

Pablo followed without letting go of her hand.

The bedroom was lit only by the soft glow of a bedside lamp, casting long shadows across the rumpled sheets.

They stood facing each other, both breathing a little unsteadily from that kiss.

Pablo searched her eyes. "Are we really doing this?" he whispered, just to be sure—giving her one last chance to back out.

Bianca cupped his face gently, brushing her thumb across his bottom lip. "Only if you want to," she whispered back, her eyes never leaving his.

He responded by gently pulling down the zipper at the back of her dress. She unbuttoned the first few buttons of his shirt, her fingers trembling ever so slightly. He swallowed hard, carefully sliding the delicate straps of her dress off her shoulders, gradually easing the silky fabric down.

The dress slipped to the floor in a whisper of satin.

His breath caught. "You're perfect," he murmured, eyes roaming her appreciatively.

She flushed under his gaze, then gave him another kiss—this one hungry and urgent as they fell back onto the bed together.

Nothing about that night was hurried, though. It wasn't just passion—it was slow, exploring, memorizing. It was tender—like they had all the time in the world. Every touch, every whisper was an echo of the journey that had brought them here.

When it was over, Bianca lay draped against Pablo's chest, her head rising and falling with his breathing.

His arm was wrapped around her, holding her close. The quiet of the night settled around them.

As she listened to the steady thump of his heart under her ear, Bianca realized something profound.

This wasn't a fling.

This wasn't just a bit of fun.

This was different. It felt different.

And that terrified her as much as it thrilled her.

Chapter Twelve: Too Close, Too Fast

Bianca lay with her head on Pablo's chest, listening to the slow rhythm of his heartbeat. His arm rested over her waist, his fingertips absentmindedly tracing small circles on her bare skin. By all rights, she should have felt content, at peace—even happy.

Instead, a cold wave of fear washed over her.

How did this happen? she wondered, her mind racing even as she remained still against him.

This wasn't part of the plan. They were supposed to be having fun—keeping things casual. No strings. No messy emotions.

And yet... here she was, wrapped up in Pablo's arms, feeling things she had sworn she wouldn't let herself feel.

She squeezed her eyes shut. She was his chef. He was a footballer, —one of the most famous young athletes in the world and for now her boss. He was nearly recovered too; soon he'd be back on the field, traveling, caught up in the glamor and chaos of his career. Surrounded by beautiful people who would throw themselves at him without a second thought.

And she... she would go back to being just his chef. The

girl who made his meals and left his kitchen spotless. There was a natural order to things, and this moment— this beautiful, fragile moment—was temporary at best, a mistake at worst.

Bianca's heart began to race with anxiety. She couldn't do this. She couldn't let herself fall for him only to watch him move on when he returned to his real life.

The realization hit so hard that she sat up abruptly, clutching the sheet to her chest. Pablo stirred beside her, still half-asleep, reaching for her instinctively.

"Bia?" he mumbled, voice heavy with exhaustion. "What's wrong?"

"I... nothing. I just—" She didn't have an excuse. Her thoughts were too loud in her head to form coherent words. She slid out of the bed quickly, wrapping the sheet around herself, and hurried into the bathroom, shutting the door with a soft click.

Pablo frowned, sitting up fully now, sleep vanishing from his eyes. Moments ago, she had been lying peacefully in his arms—now she was practically running away. Something wasn't right.

Inside the bathroom, Bianca gripped the marble sink, trying to steady her breathing. In the mirror, she saw her reflection—flushed cheeks, swollen lips, hair a wild mess from his hands. She looked different.

Like a woman who had just made a huge mistake.

Not because she regretted what happened. But because she had allowed herself to get too close, too fast.

She squeezed her eyes shut. This is why she never let herself get distracted—why she focused on work, on goals, on things she could control. Because letting someone in like this meant giving them the power to hurt her.

And Pablo easily had that power now.

She could already picture how this might go: he'd heal completely, go back to his life under the spotlight, and eventually... this thing between them would fade for him. He'd meet someone else—someone who fit into his world better, perhaps a model or actress—or simply move on when the season of training and travel made their arrangement inconvenient. And she'd be left picking up the pieces of her own heart, having possibly lost not only a lover but a client and friend as well.

No. She couldn't let that happen.

Out in the bedroom, Pablo gently knocked on the bathroom door. "Bia? You okay?" His voice was soft but concerned.

She swallowed hard, determined to get through this with her dignity intact. "Yeah! I'm fine," she called, forcing her voice to sound as normal as possible. "I just... needed a second."

Pablo's frown deepened. She didn't sound fine. She sounded like someone trying very hard to appear fine.

"Can we talk?" he asked quietly through the door.

Bianca's mind raced. Talk. Right. She should talk to him —tell him what she was feeling, maybe. But the thought of admitting those vulnerabilities horrified her. She wasn't ready to say out loud that she was already halfway to falling in love with him.

"Uh, sure. Give me a minute."

He wasn't convinced, but he stepped back and waited,

running a hand through his tousled hair.

Inside, Bianca splashed cool water on her face. She could do this. Keep it together. She adjusted the sheet around her and tried to steady her features into neutrality before opening the door.

Pablo was standing right there, wearing only his boxer briefs, worry etched on his face. Seeing him—hair mussed, concern in those green eyes she adored—nearly broke her resolve. She hesitated, and he immediately noticed her guarded posture.

"You're scared," he said softly, searching her face.

She opened her mouth, but nothing came out.

"Tell me why," he pressed gently.

She shook her head, stepping past him and quickly gathering her scattered clothes from the floor, clutching them to her chest as if they were armour. "It doesn't matter," she said, avoiding his gaze. "I should go. It's late and—"

Pablo moved to block her path to the door, not touching her but standing firmly in front of her. "Bianca, please."

Her name on his lips like that—it was soft, almost pleading. She couldn't meet his eyes, focusing instead on his chest, on the steady rise and fall of his breathing.

"You're scared," he repeated, his voice quiet but resolute. "Tell me why."

She clenched her jaw, her eyes burning suddenly with unshed tears of stress and confusion. "This... this wasn't supposed to happen," she managed, her voice tight.

"What wasn't?"

"This." She gestured between them, then at the bed, frustrated and flustered. "All of this. We were supposed to keep it professional or, at most, casual. No feelings, no complications."

Pablo's brow furrowed. "And you think we've messed that up?"

She let out a short, humourless laugh. "Haven't we? You're nearly finished with your recovery. You'll be traveling again, back to your real life—models in your DMs, late-night parties after wins, all of that. I'll go back to being your chef, and... and you'll move on." She swallowed the lump in her throat. "I was never supposed to be more than a temporary distraction for you, Pablo. The problem is I fell hard and it is my fault not yours."

The words hung in the air, and saying them out loud nearly broke her heart. She hadn't realized until now how deeply that fear ran.

Pablo looked like she'd slapped him. "You think that's all this is?" he asked, an edge to his voice—hurt and a little angry. "A distraction?"

She hugged her clothes to herself. "Isn't it? We agreed, simple, no strings attached and I just became too attached."

His jaw tightened. He stepped closer, and she backed up until she felt the cool wall against her bare shoulders. His face was intense, eyes burning into hers. "You really think I could just forget about you and that I am not feeling the same things you are?" he asked, almost incredulously.

She opened her mouth, but no sound came.

He shook his head in disbelief. "You think I'd just go back to my life and... what? Pretend you don't exist?

That none of this meant anything?"

She looked away, guilt and fear warring inside her. When she didn't answer, he huffed in frustration.

"I don't care about casual, Bianca. I don't care about rules or what we said before. All I know is that when you walked into my life, everything changed. And I don't want to go back to how it was." Her eyes flicked to his face, surprised by the raw sincerity she heard.

He took another step, and now he tipped her chin up gently with his fingers, forcing her to look at him. "I don't want 'just fun' with you, Bianca. Simple and no strings attached has gone out of the window a long ago"

She felt tears prickling at the corners of her eyes. She blinked rapidly, not wanting them to fall. "Pablo..."

"You mean more to me than that. A lot more."

Her breath caught. This was exactly what she had secretly longed to hear and exactly what terrified her to her core.

She had convinced herself he didn't feel the same because thinking otherwise was too dangerous—too painful to hope for.

She opened her mouth, still unsure what to say.

He beat her to it.

"I want you," he said softly but firmly. "Not just for tonight. Not just as a friend or my chef."

She froze, stunned by the straightforward declaration.

He ran a hand through his hair and continued, his tone almost angry at her assumption. "I don't care about casual. I don't care about complications. All I know is that with you everything is better. And I don't want to lose that. I don't want to lose you." Bianca stared at him, stunned into silence.

"I want you to be my girlfriend, Bia." He said.

She couldn't believe what she was hearing.

He gentled his voice when she didn't respond. Lifting a hand, he cupped her cheek, brushing away one tear that had escaped. "Tell me you don't feel the same, and I'll drop it," he said quietly. "I swear. We'll chalk it up to the heat of the moment, or loneliness, or whatever you want, and go back to exactly how things were. I won't ever mention it again."

Her lips parted, but the words wouldn't come. Because they would be lying, and they both knew it.

He searched her eyes. His thumb stroked her cheek softly, wiping another tear. "Then stay and let's try this."

Her heart thundered in her chest.

He leaned in, lips hovering just inches from hers, giving her the chance to pull away if she wanted.

She didn't.

Instead, she closed the remaining distance, kissing him with all the longing she'd held back for too long.

In that moment, she surrendered—to her feelings, to this connection between them she had tried so hard to deny.

And she knew—this wasn't temporary.

This was real.

Chapter Thirteen: No More Games And The Unwelcome Surprise

Six months had passed since that night when everything changed—since that night that turned their relationship into something neither of them could have imagined when they had their first video call nearly a year ago.

Bianca and Pablo had settled into a rhythm in the time since—no longer just as chef and footballer but also as a couple navigating something new, delicate, and very real. They tried to keep the relationship to themselves for now. It was Bia's choice as she just didn't have the energy yet to make it public and deal with all that would come dating a famous person like Pablo.

It wasn't always easy. Balancing their individual goals with this budding love required a careful dance of understanding and compromise. Some days felt effortless —like when she'd cook a new dish and he'd twirl her around the kitchen in delight, or when he'd come home from physio and they'd slow dance in the living room to old Brazilian love songs, dinner forgotten on the stove. Other days felt like walking a tightrope—managing schedules, work, and their own fears.

But somehow, they made it work.

Bianca still cooked four days a week for him, but now meals were shared at the table rather than left in the fridge. Sometimes, she'd sit cross-legged on the kitchen counter telling him about her day while he clumsily chopped vegetables at her side. Other nights, they'd abandon the cooking entirely to curl up on the couch together, takeout containers on the coffee table, her head on his shoulder as they watched cooking shows she critiqued mercilessly.

Pablo was happier than he had been in a long time. His knee was healing perfectly—ahead of schedule, his doctors said. With Bianca's presence, even his soul felt lighter. Training was no longer just about getting back to football; it was about returning to his full life—a life that now included her in ways he'd never anticipated.

And Bianca? She tried—she really tried—not to overthink how deeply she had fallen for him.

But there were moments when the reality of their situation would hit her. She'd catch him looking at her from across the room, his eyes soft with an emotion that made her chest ache, and she knew this was something precious and real. This was something worth protecting, worth fighting for.

Now, with Pablo's return to football around the corner, everything was about to shift again.

"This will change things, won't it?" Bianca asked quietly one night. They were sprawled on his sofa, her head on his chest, the TV playing some action movie neither of them was watching. Outside, rain pattered against the windows, creating a cocoon of warmth and intimacy inside.

He glanced down at her, his fingers gently combing through her hair. "What do you mean?"

"You, going back. The games. The travel. The press. The cameras. The scrutiny... us," she said softly, voicing the fears that had been growing as his return date approached.

Pablo exhaled slowly. "I've thought about that too. A lot, actually."

Bianca pushed herself up a little so she could see his face. "Do you think we're ready? For people to know about us?"

He looked into her eyes, his own reflecting both certainty and understanding of her hesitation. "I don't know," he admitted honestly. "But I do know I want you there with me. When I walk back onto that field for the first time... I want people to know who's been by my side through it all. I don't want to hide this— hide us—like it's something wrong."

Bianca felt a flutter in her chest and smiled, albeit nervously. "You sure? It's not just going to be about your comeback then. The press will dig—into you, into me. Into how we met, what I'm doing with someone like you."

"Let them," he said, more firmly than she expected. "I have nothing to hide."

She looked away, biting her lip. "Pablo... I'm not used to all of this. I just wanted to be a chef. Not someone people Google as a footballer's girlfriend."

He reached out, cupping her cheek. "And you still are. And you are also my partner... and if people have something to say about it, they can take it up with me."

She chuckled. "You sound like a bodyguard."

"I can be scary," he said with a mock-serious tone, puffing up his chest.

Bianca laughed, poking him in the ribs. "Please. You cried when we watched The Lion King last week for the millionth time."

"It's very emotional!" he protested, grinning.

The laughter eased the tension, but they both recognized the unspoken reality—they were venturing into uncharted waters together. Neither had navigated a serious relationship before, and with Pablo's fame ensuring media scrutiny of his every move, their path forward wouldn't be simple. They couldn't have anticipated just how turbulent this journey would become.

A few days later, the news leaked. First, a blurry photo of them leaving that restaurant event surfaced on a gossip site. Then another, clearer one of them walking hand-in-hand out of his building on a morning when he had training and she was heading to the market.

Within hours, it was everywhere.

"Brazilian football star Pablo Costa seen with mystery woman in London."

"Mystery woman identified as his personal chef—Bianca Almeida."

Her phone buzzed non-stop for two days. Her social media following exploded. Requests for interviews and cooking segments poured into her email. Her email crashed twice from the influx.

Not everything was positive. There were nasty comments in the mix. Questions about her motives. Accusations that she was trying to "trap" a footballer. One tabloid even dug up an old photo of her hugging a male friend from culinary school years ago and spun it into a silly scandal.

She sat in Pablo's kitchen one morning, scrolling through her phone with a knot in her stomach. "Don't people have anything better to do?" she muttered, turning the screen face-down on the counter.

Pablo walked in, freshly showered, barefoot and still in gym shorts. He frowned when he saw her expression. "What happened?"

She hesitated, but then sighed, deciding honesty was easier. "They found an old photo of me with Gabriel

—from my culinary school. Apparently, now I 'dated multiple famous men.'"

He raised an eyebrow. "Gabriel? The chef that dates your cousin Ricardo? The one with the man bun and the cat named Beyoncé?"

She nodded, unable to suppress a little laugh. "Yes. But the internet doesn't care about context or finding the truth."

Pablo came over and wrapped his arms around her from behind. "Then let them talk. We know the truth.

That's what matters."

She leaned back into his warmth, letting the stress ebb away just a bit. "You really don't care what they say?"

"Not if it means I get to kiss you good morning and goodnight every day," he said softly.

Her heart melted a little at that.

And so, they braced themselves for what was to come— new fame, new challenges, a brighter spotlight than either had asked for. And their parents at some point which Bia didn't want to even think about for now. She kept changing subjects when her mum asked if it was true what she read in the news about them.

Chapter Fourteen: Truth Revealed

One evening, Bianca sat on Pablo's couch, her legs tucked in, scrolling through her phone. Pablo lay beside her, resting his head in her lap, absently scrolling through his own.

"So..." Pablo broke the silence, his voice casual. "My parents are coming next week for my first game back."

Bianca paused her scrolling, her fingers stopping mid-swipe. "Oh? That's nice. You must be excited to see them."

Pablo nodded but seemed distracted. He tilted his head to meet her gaze. "Yeah, but, uh... here's the thing."

Bianca raised an eyebrow. "That sounds like a setup for bad news."

He smirked, shaking his head. "Not bad news. Just... an interesting idea." He hesitated for a moment, then dropped his voice slightly. "Your parents are coming too, right?" Bianca blinked, clearly caught off guard. "Yeah, but how do you---"

"You told me last week, remember?" He grinned, his eyes twinkling.

She frowned, trying to remember. "Oh. Right. I did. But don't worry we will get out of your feet. I plan on taking them to visit famous places and all."

He sat up, stretching his arms and giving her a playful look. "Well, I was thinking... Since they're all going to be here at the same time, why don't we introduce them? You know, make it official."

Bianca froze; phone forgotten in her hand. "Introduce them? As in, like, meet each other? And tell them about us?"

"Yeah. We're kind of a thing now, Bianca. And, well, they're going to find out soon enough anyway— might as well beat the media to it." He leaned closer, brushing a stray strand of hair behind her ear. "It'll be good to just get it out in the open, you know?"

Bianca's heart rate picked up, a mixture of nerves and excitement flooding her. "But what if they don't take it well? Especially that they have seen the news around, and we haven't actually told them the truth ourselves"

Pablo raised an eyebrow and smiled softly. "Don't be dramatic. They like us both, don't they? I mean, they know each other, even if it's in different contexts."

"I know," she replied slowly. "But liking us separately and then approving of us as a couple are two different things."

Pablo chuckled, rolling his eyes playfully. "Oh, come on. You're seriously telling me they're going to have an issue with *this*?" He gestured between the two of them. "We're cute together, right?"

Bianca bit her lip, trying to ignore the anxiety creeping in. "I don't know... It's not just about us. It's about everything surrounding us. You're a footballer. I'm—well, I'm not sure where I fit into this whole 'public eye' thing. What if they think this is just... messy? I know for sure my dad is not going to like it. Footballers have a bad reputation, you know that!"

Pablo's smile, and he reached out to touch her arm gently. "We'll handle it. Whatever happens, we'll handle it together. Besides, I play for your dad's favourite team in the premier league, I will just promise him I will score every game."

She sighed and laughed. "Yeah, sure that's going to work!"

She continued: "But for real now, they are going to have their own thoughts, their own worries."

"True," he said thoughtfully. "But we won't know unless we do it. We can introduce them as a couple before the paparazzi makes it official. And hey, maybe we can even have a few laughs at the awkwardness."

Bianca let out a nervous laugh. "Sure, because meeting your family and mine is *totally* going to be filled with laughs."

Pablo smiled, pulling her closer so she was almost leaning against him. "We've survived worse, haven't we?"

She hesitated for a moment, before leaning into his side, finally giving in. "Fine. Let's do it. We'll introduce them."

Pablo grinned. "Deal. Just promise me you won't pass out from the nerves in front of them."

Bianca raised an eyebrow. "I promise nothing."

"Oh man," he said, wrapping his arms around her in a tight hug. "I'll make sure to have some backup plans in case they start grilling us. And, worst case, we can always blame it on the media."

She smirked, looking up at him. "And who's going to blame it on the media when they ask why you two are always seen together now?"

He laughed. "We'll figure it out."

Chapter Fifteen: The Meeting

The dinner was set for the following weekend at Pablo's house. The air inside felt thick with anticipation as they made final preparations.

His parents arrived first. Isabella—his mother—swept in like a queen, elegant and sharp-eyed, taking in everything with a knowing smile. Her gaze landed on Bianca with a slight, knowing curve of her lips that made Bianca's stomach flutter. His father, Ricardo, followed closely, tall and serious. He shook Bianca's hand in a way that was polite but devoid of much warmth—a measured greeting rather than a friendly one.

Bianca's parents arrived shortly after. Her mother, Camila, immediately enveloped everyone in hugs, her infectious laughter filling any gap of silence. Her father, Marco, hung back a bit protectively, observing quietly, his presence a subtle shield at Bianca's side.

The evening began smoothly enough. Over appetizers and small talk, everyone shared stories—Isabella delighted in recounting a tale from Pablo's childhood when he accidentally kicked a football through a neighbour's window; Camila countered with a story of Bianca as a little girl, concocting "perfume" out of rose petals and vinegar that stunk up their entire house. There was laughter, a sense of cautious ease.

But halfway through dinner, something shifted.

Ricardo set down his fork and cleared his throat, drawing all eyes. His gaze moved to Bianca. "So, you're Pablo's personal chef, right?"

Bianca nodded, keeping her voice steady. "Yes, that's right."

Isabella's lips curled in a polite smile that nevertheless carried a touch of scrutiny. "He always talks about your food. Says it's the best he's ever had."

Pablo grinned wide. "It's true. I'm never eating anyone else's cooking again. You're stuck with me, Bianca."

Camila chuckled warmly. "It's been so nice to hear how much respect Pablo has for you—not just as his chef, but as a friend," she said, patting Bianca's hand.

Bianca felt warmth from the compliment, but caught a flicker of unease in Pablo's eyes at how this conversation might unfold.

Pablo's expression grew a little tense. He clearly sensed the rising pressure in the room, just as she did.

Marco, usually a man of few words, nodded at Camila's statement. "Yes, she always talks about you when she calls. We've always thought it was great that she works for someone respectful."

"Uh... yeah..." Bianca cleared her throat, unsure where this was leading.

Pablo's mother tilted her head, her eyes narrowing slightly as she looked between Pablo and Bianca. "You never mentioned anything more than friendship, either," she remarked softly but pointedly.

The words hung in the air. Bianca's heart quickened. She

hadn't expected this to come out so soon, certainly not in front of everyone, but here they were, toeing the line.

Pablo sighed, placing his fork down and meeting the eyes now all on them. He reached over and laced his fingers with Bianca's on the table. "Well, that's because we weren't ready to say anything yet."

Isabella's gaze sharpened, though her expression remained unreadable. "Say anything about what?"

Pablo turned to Bianca and without another thought, interlocked their fingers visibly on the table. "That we're together. As in, dating." Silence.

The air felt thick as those words landed, heavy and undeniable. Bianca's throat tightened; this was it—the moment where everything could change.

Ricardo's face remained stoic as he spoke low, "Together... as in a relationship?"

Pablo nodded, jaw set. "Yes. We've been seeing each other for a while now." Another beat of heavy silence.

Isabella exhaled through her nose; her expression unreadable. "Pablo..." she began, her tone hard to gauge.

Bianca's father shifted in his seat, brow furrowing. "Bianca..."

Bianca felt her heart hammering against her ribs. "What?" she asked, her voice betraying the uncertainty she suddenly felt.

Camila, always the gentle mediator, leaned forward, her voice calm and steady. "We love you both. You know that."

"But..." Ricardo interrupted, his tone firm. "But this is not the time for a relationship."

Bianca felt her stomach twist with something cold. This was exactly the conversation she had dreaded.

Her eyes flicked to Pablo, expecting to see hesitation or doubt in his face—perhaps worry now that their families voiced concerns. Instead, she saw determination. A fire in his eyes she hadn't seen before. He squeezed her hand under the table, as if telling her he wasn't letting go.

Pablo looked directly at his parents, his voice calm but with tension thrumming beneath. "So what? You want us to break up?"

Ricardo's gaze didn't waver. "We're saying... think about what's best for your futures."

Bianca's breath hitched, a weight settling in her stomach. Was this the right time? Was she doing the right thing?

But then Pablo turned to her, squeezing her hand, and she realized—this was no longer about the "right time." It was about them, what they were willing to fight for.

"I don't care what anyone thinks," he said, voice low but filled with raw sincerity. He looked straight into her eyes. "I want to be with you, Bianca. Nothing's going to change that." Her heart skipped a beat as she stared back into those earnest green eyes.

This wasn't just a test of their relationship; this was a test of their courage.

Bianca swallowed the lump in her throat and, with trembling resolve, she turned to face the table of concerned parents. "Me too," she said, her voice coming out stronger than she felt. "I want to be with Pablo. We're happy together. We know what we're doing."

The room went still, as if the world held its breath. All eyes were on them, waiting for the inevitable judgment.

But with Pablo's hand firmly holding hers, Bianca knew one thing: They would figure it out. Together.

The tension was palpable. Bianca felt Pablo's warm hand clasping hers under the table, a lifeline anchoring her through the weight of the conversation.

Her father, Marco, was the first to break the silence that followed their joint declaration. He cleared his throat, voice steady but edged with worry. "Bianca... you've always been ambitious. You worked so hard to get here. We just don't want to see you throw away your dreams for a relationship."

Bianca felt a knot tighten in her chest. She understood her parents' concern—they didn't want her to lose sight of her goals. But the way it sounded, it was as if they were accusing her of doing exactly that by being with Pablo. "Why does being with Pablo mean throwing away my dreams?" she asked defensively, her words sharper than she intended.

Her mother, Camila, leaned forward, eyes soft but lined with concern. "Darling, you know how relationships can be. They take time, effort, and hard work. And Pablo—" she shot an apologetic glance at him, "—he's about to travel again, and be in the public eye more than ever. That world is demanding. Are you ready for that?" Her voice trembled slightly with her own fear for her daughter.

Bianca's gaze shifted to Pablo without even realizing it. He was watching her, concerned in his eyes too— but she also saw that unwavering support. The world they were talking about *was* his world. But she wasn't a stranger to hard work. She had built her life, and she wasn't about to let anyone dictate her happiness now.

Before she could muster a response, Pablo's father cleared his throat. "And you, Pablo? You're finally returning to football. The media will be all over you. A public relationship can bring unnecessary distractions. We're just worried."

Pablo exhaled, the frustration flickering across his face. "I understand your concerns, really, I do. But this isn't just some fling. Bianca and I... we balance each other. We push each other to be better."

Bianca nodded, adding quickly, "My career isn't going anywhere. I love what I do, and being with Pablo doesn't change that. He respects my work, just like I respect his."

She turned to look at him, eyes searching his. "And I know his career is his priority. I would never hold him back from that."

Pablo squeezed her hand, his grip firm and reassuring. "And I would never hold her back either. We can support each other and still chase our dreams," he said confidently.

A thick silence followed as the weight of their words settled. All parties were holding their breath, waiting for the next move.

Finally, Isabella folded her hands on the table and addressed them, a mix of caution and something almost like curiosity in her gaze. "You both sound serious about this."

Pablo didn't break eye contact with his mother. "We are."

Camila looked at Bianca, her eyes moist though she smiled gently. "And, you're sure? You're ready for everything that comes with this?" Her voice was quieter now, not challenging but truly asking—for reassurance, perhaps, or for her own peace of mind.

Bianca swallowed hard, then nodded more to herself than anyone else. "Yes. I've never been surer about anything."

Another silence, but this one felt slightly different—less charged, more contemplative.

Marco leaned back in his chair, his gaze still on them. "You both seem certain," he said, voice lower now. "But you also need to promise us something."

Bianca's heart skipped nervously. "What now?" she asked quietly.

Her father exchanged a look with her mother, then cleared his throat. "Promise us that you will stay focused on your careers too. No distractions, no losing yourselves in this relationship. If you truly care for each other, you'll help each other succeed, not become each other's excuse to fail."

Bianca's stomach dropped. It was a valid point—she understood it well. And the last thing she wanted was to lose herself in something that could derail everything she had worked for. But the look in Pablo's eyes gave her strength. She wouldn't let that happen; neither would he.

Pablo broke into a slow smile, relief and confidence returning. "Deal," he said immediately. "I wouldn't want anything else."

Bianca matched his smile, her eyes shining with gratitude and resolve. "Neither would I."

The room seemed to collectively exhale, the heavy atmosphere beginning to lift. Camila reached over and placed her hand over Bianca's, her fingers warm and comforting. "Then we're happy for you, honey," she said, her voice filled with love.

Isabella, still cautious, gave a small, measured smile. "Just take care of each other, okay?"

Pablo's grin widened. "Always."

And with that, the rest of the evening flowed more easily. Conversation turned lighter—childhood memories, playful teasing, stories of Pablo's and Bianca's respective journeys that had everyone giggling. It was a stark contrast to the intense moments earlier, but a welcome relief. Still, as Bianca glanced over at Pablo across the table during a round of laughter, her heart swelled with something new—hope.

As the evening drew to a close, one realization settled deep in Bianca's mind: this was just the beginning. Not just for her and Pablo, but for everything. The path they had chosen wouldn't be easy, but they had the most important thing—their unwavering support for each other. And if they could make it through *this*, they could make it through anything.

The next few days, Bianca would spend the day visiting places with her parents and evenings they would all eat together at Pablo's place.

Chapter Sixteen: The Big Day

The comeback day arrived. The stadium buzzed with anticipation. Fans filled the stands, waving banners and chanting Pablo's name. It had been over six months since he last stepped onto the field, and today was the moment everyone had been waiting for—his grand return.

Bianca sat nervously in the VIP section, her hands gripping the edge of her seat. Beside her, both their families sat together, a united front despite their initial doubts. She could feel their excitement, but she could also sense the weight of what this day meant—not just for Pablo, but for them as a couple.

Pablo had told her last night, his voice full of conviction, "*Tomorrow, the world will know. No more hiding, no more pretending. If they want to talk, let them talk. You're my girlfriend, and I'm proud of that.*" And he had meant it.

As the players began to emerge from the tunnel, the roar of the crowd was deafening. Pablo was the last to step onto the field, his number flashing across the big screen.

The entire stadium erupted.

The moment was surreal. Bianca watched as Pablo looked up towards the VIP section, his eyes locking with hers, and for a brief second, it was as if it was just the two of them in the entire world. He smiled, gave her a subtle nod, and she knew—this wasn't just a comeback for him. This was their moment. And then, the cameras turned to her.

Flashes went off in every direction. Photographers zoomed in on her, and Bianca's phone vibrated endlessly with notifications.

"Who is she?"

"Meet Pablo Costa's New Girlfriend—The Mystery Woman in the Stands!"

"Pablo's Big Return... And His Big Announcement?"

She saw her face on the stadium screens as the broadcasters introduced her:

"That's Bianca Almeida, the Brazilian chef who has stolen Pablo Costa's heart! Until now, she's been known as his personal chef, but it looks like she's much more than that!"

Pablo's mother, Isabella, leaned over and whispered, *"Are you ready for this, darling? Because it's just the beginning."*

Bianca swallowed, trying to steady her nerves. She had never imagined herself in this world—the world of flashing cameras, magazine headlines, and paparazzi. She was used to cooking in kitchens, not sitting in a stadium while the world dissected her every move.

Still, when she looked back at the field and saw Pablo standing tall, focused, and determined, she knew she had no regrets.

She was here. With him.

And no matter what the media said, she wasn't going anywhere.

Chapter Seventeen: A Year of Love and a Proposal for Forever

The past year had been a whirlwind for both Bianca and Pablo. Their relationship, once private and simple, had been thrust into the public eye with the subtlety of a fireworks display.

"Have you seen this?" Bianca had asked one morning, sliding her phone across the kitchen counter where

Pablo was nursing his pre-training espresso. Another tabloid headline: "Chef Captures Footballer's Heart —And Appetite!"

Pablo had merely grinned, that gorgeous smile that still made her heart skip a beat. "At least they got the appetite right," he'd quipped, eyeing the homemade breakfast spread before him.

But despite the pressure, the media scrutiny, and their demanding careers, they had managed to grow stronger together—perhaps because of these challenges rather than in spite of them.

Pablo was thriving on the field—his comeback season had been one of the best of his career, with goals, assists, and trophies piling up like autumn leaves. The sports commentators who had once written him off after his injury were now singing his praises, calling it "The Bianca Effect." Pablo never corrected them.

Bianca, meanwhile, had transformed her newfound fame into opportunity, launching her own private catering business, cooking for celebrities, athletes, and high-profile clients in London. What had started as a whispered recommendation among Pablo's teammates had exploded into a waiting list three months long. She had even begun filming a series of online cooking tutorials that gained a devoted following, her natural warmth and no-nonsense approach cutting through the digital noise.

"You make it look so easy," Pablo had told her once, after watching her expertly dice an onion without shedding a single tear.

"Says the man who can bend a football around a wall of defenders with his eyes closed," she'd retorted, but the pride in her eyes betrayed her casual tone.

They travelled together when schedules allowed. Weekend escapes to the countryside, where no one recognized them and they could hold hands without seeing it on Instagram the next day. Spontaneous trips to Italy, where Bianca would charm local chefs into revealing generations-old secrets, and Pablo would attempt to translate with his broken Italian, resulting in fits of laughter and unexpected culinary discoveries. Cozy nights at home watching movies, debating plotlines, and occasionally falling asleep halfway through, exhausted from their respective demanding days.

Life moved at a breakneck pace, but they always made time for each other. Morning coffee rituals, late night phone calls when apart, surprise lunches at training grounds, and post-match dinners where Pablo would dissect his performance and Bianca would listen, understanding more about the beautiful game with each passing week.

And now, a year later, Pablo had decided.

It was time.

The small velvet box had been burning a hole in his sock drawer for weeks. He'd nearly shown it to her a dozen times —after a particularly perfect dinner she'd cooked, during sunset on their balcony, in the middle of the night when he'd woken up just to watch her sleeping peacefully beside him. But something had always held him back. Not doubt, never doubt. He wanted the moment to be... what was that word Bianca always used when plating her dishes? Perfect balance.

Tonight, he thought as he laced up his boots for the biggest game of the season, might just offer that balance.

Chapter Eighteen: The Final Score

The stadium was packed to capacity, a sea of team colours undulating with every near-miss and skilful play. Fans were chanting Pablo's name with a fervour that rattled the rafters, the sound reverberating through the concrete and steel like a heartbeat.

It was the final game of the season, and his team needed just one goal to secure the championship. Ninety minutes to immortality. Ninety minutes to make history—or to crumble under the weight of expectation.

Bianca sat in the VIP section, surrounded by their families who had flown in "for the big game," Pablo had said, though his eyes had told a different story. Isabella, Pablo's mother, kept squeezing Bianca's hand at random intervals, an inexplicable gleam in her eye. Ricardo, his father, seemed unusually interested in the ring finger of Bianca's left hand, his gaze darting away whenever she caught him looking.

She felt butterflies in her stomach—not just because of the game but because something felt different about tonight. Pablo had been quieter than usual that morning, his kiss goodbye lingering longer than normal. He'd held her face in his hands, studying her features as if memorizing them for a test.

"What?" she'd laughed nervously.

"Nothing," he'd replied. "Everything."

The first half ended scoreless, tense. The second half began with mounting pressure, Pablo narrowly missing two chances that left him pounding the turf in frustration. Bianca could read his body language like a recipe she'd memorized—the set of his shoulders, the way he tugged at his captain's armband, the glances toward the coach.

Time was running out. Substitutions were made. Tactical shifts implemented. The stadium held its collective breath as the minutes ticked away.

Then, in the 75th minute, it happened.

A perfect pass came Pablo's way, threading between two defenders like a needle. The stadium inhaled as one. Time seemed to slow as Pablo controlled the ball with one exquisite touch, his body positioning already perfect. He looked up for a split second, measuring, calculating, feeling rather than thinking.

The goalkeeper shifted his weight, revealing just a sliver of the top corner. It was all Pablo needed.

He curled a stunning shot that seemed to bend against the laws of physics, the ball spinning and dipping in a beautiful arc before nestling into the top corner of the net with a satisfying ripple.

GOOOOOAL!

The stadium erupted, a volcano of noise and celebration. His teammates sprinted toward him, faces twisted in jubilation. The coach leapt from the bench, assistants embracing wildly beside him.

Pablo ran across the field, celebrating—but not in the usual way.

Instead of his signature fist-pump that had graced countless highlight reels, he ran toward the stands, straight to where Bianca sat, her hands clasped over her mouth in disbelief and joy.

Confusion rippled through the crowd. This wasn't in the celebration playbook. The referee, whistle halfway to his lips to restart play, paused, sensing something extraordinary unfolding.

Pablo reached into his sock—not the one with his shin guard, but the other—and pulled out a small black velvet box that had somehow survived ninety minutes of elite athletic competition. Without hesitation, without regard for the millions watching globally, without a second thought for the championship still technically hanging in the balance, he dropped to one knee right in front of the entire world.

The crowd went wild, understanding dawning in waves across the stadium as the jumbotron camera operator, quick-witted and romantic, swung the lens toward this unfolding drama.

Bianca's hands shot up to her mouth, tears already filling her eyes as realization crashed over her. Every strange interaction of the past week suddenly made perfect sense —his parents' unexpected visit, his teammates' knowing glances at the pre-game dinner, his uncharacteristic nervousness this morning.

The cameras zoomed in, broadcasting the moment to millions across continents and time zones, sports bars erupting in romantic sighs, living rooms filled with unexpected tears.

With his heart racing—from exertion, from fear, from

love so overwhelming it threatened to burst from his chest—Pablo looked up at her, his trademark confidence momentarily wavering before steadying into a smile that was just for her, even in this most public of moments.

"Bianca Almeida," he began, his voice somehow carrying through the cacophony, *"you've been feeding my soul since the day we met. When I score goals, they're for the team. But when I come home, it's only for you. You are the championship I want to win every day for the rest of my life."* He took a breath and opened the box to reveal a ring that caught the stadium lights in a dance of fire. *"Will you marry me?"*

She didn't even hesitate; she didn't need the extra second to think that she took when deciding between olive oils or choosing which spice to add.

"YES!" she shouted, nodding furiously as she threw herself over the barricade and into his arms, nearly toppling them both onto the pristine turf.

The stadium exploded into cheers that threatened to lift the roof. His teammates ran over, lifting the newly engaged couple up as if they'd just scored the winning goal in the World Cup final.

Bianca laughed through her tears, one hand clinging onto the love of her life, the other stretched out, admiring how the diamond caught the light. Someone—was it the team captain?—was already uncorking champagne, breaking about fifteen stadium regulations in the process.

The referee, a notorious stickler for rules, made a show of looking at his watch before breaking into a grin and gesturing that perhaps the remaining fifteen minutes could wait just a moment longer.

The world had just witnessed not only a championship-winning goal...

But the beginning of their forever.

And in the press box, journalists were already rewriting their headlines because sometimes, just sometimes, love was an even bigger story than sports.

Chapter Nineteen: A Forever Kind of Love

The waves crashed gently against the shore, the golden sunset casting a warm glow over the pristine beaches of Rio de Janeiro. The air was soft with salt and promise. Gentle acoustic guitar music drifted through the breeze, blending effortlessly with the rhythm of the ocean.

It was the perfect day. The kind of day that felt like magic was sewn into the sky.

Bianca stood in front of the mirror inside a small beachside villa, her heart thudding in her chest—not from nerves but from the weight of joy. Her white lace gown flowed around her like ocean foam, delicate and radiant. Her hair, curled in soft waves, was pinned loosely with white orchids, and her eyes sparkled with tears she hadn't let fall yet.

Behind her, Camila dabbed the corner of her own eyes. "You've never looked more like yourself than you do right now."

Bianca turned to her mother, eyes shining. "I didn't think I'd be this calm."

Camila smiled gently. "That's how you know it's right."

A soft knock on the door announced Elena, wearing a soft

blue bridesmaid's dress, her smile radiant. "It's time. Your father is waiting outside. He's trying very hard not to cry but failing miserably."

Bianca took a deep breath, smoothing her hands over her dress one last time. This journey that had begun with a business contract was about to transform into something eternal.

Outside, Pablo stood barefoot in the sand, the sleeves of his white linen shirt rolled up, his skin golden from the sun. He looked out toward the ocean, running his hand through his dark hair, trying to settle the racing in his chest.

His best man nudged him. "You alright, bro?"

Pablo gave a shaky laugh. "I'm about to marry the woman who makes the best feijoada and stole my heart. I've never been better."

Laughter rippled through the small crowd. Pablo's eyes found Bianca's mum in the front row. Camila, elegant and composed, gave him a warm smile. Next to her sat his parents, beaming with pride. How far they had come from those first awkward family dinners.

And then—

The music shifted.

Everyone turned. There she was.

Bianca appeared at the top of the wooden walkway, her arm linked with her father's. Framed by palm trees and bathed in sunlight, she paused for a moment, her eyes finding Pablo instantly among the small gathering. Marco leaned in to whisper something that made her smile, then kissed her cheek before they began their walk.

Pablo froze. It felt like the earth tilted slightly. Like everything he had ever hoped for, it had finally, finally arrived.

His breath caught. "Wow..."

As she walked toward him, her eyes locked on his, unwavering. It felt like time folded in on itself—all the memories of burnt toast in his kitchen, stolen kisses in dark corners, fights, makeups, fears, and laughter —rushed back in one beautiful tide.

When she reached him, Marco placed Bianca's hand in Pablo's with a gentle nod—a silent passing of trust —before taking his seat beside Camila.

"You're the most beautiful thing I've ever seen," Pablo whispered.

"And you're everything I never knew I needed," she whispered back.

The ceremony was simple, intimate—barefoot on the sand, the ocean their backdrop, love their language.

Their vows were personal, spoken through tears and laughter.

"I promise," Pablo said, voice trembling, "to love you through every goal, every injury, every match won and lost. I promise to put your smile before mine and your dreams right beside mine. This is one contract I'll never want to renegotiate," he added with a smile that made their guests chuckle, remembering how it all began.

Bianca's lips quivered. "I promise to be your peace when the world gets loud. To be your strength when you need grounding. And to always, always choose you—even on the hardest days. I promise to cook for you for the rest of our lives—and to never let you crack an egg with one hand again," she added with a teary laugh.

When the officiant finally said, "You may kiss the bride," Pablo didn't hesitate. He lifted Bianca into his arms with a joyful laugh and kissed her like they were the only two people on earth.

Guests erupted in cheers as white rose petals fluttered around them, dancing on the wind like blessings.

Later that night, long after the music faded and the guests had gone, Bianca and Pablo returned to the villa lit only by candles and moonlight. The ocean murmured just outside.

She stood barefoot in the doorway, wearing his shirt now, her hair tousled, her eyes soft.

"You tired, husband?" she asked with a playful smile.

Pablo crossed the room slowly, his shirtless torso, hair slightly messy, that look of utter awe still on his face. "Not even close, wife."

They stood in silence for a moment, just looking at each other—so much was said with nothing at all.

"I still can't believe you're mine," he murmured, touching her cheek.

Bianca leaned into his hand. "You've always been mine."

Their kiss was slow, reverent, filled with the kind of love that only deepens in silence. He lifted her gently, carrying her to the bed strewn with soft linens and flower petals.

That night wasn't rushed or fiery—it was tender. Every movement, every whisper was an echo of their journey. They traced old scars and new promises. They laughed, they cried, and they held each other like nothing else existed.

And when they finally lay tangled in each other's arms, the world outside didn't matter.

It was just them. Two souls who had fought through fear, distance, and doubt—and chose each other anyway.

And tomorrow, they would begin writing the next chapter together.

Chapter Twenty: Just Us

The sun spilled in through the windows of the honeymoon suite, casting golden light across the room.

The sound of the ocean echoed faintly outside, a soft, soothing lullaby.

Bianca stirred beneath the light linen sheets, a lazy smile curving her lips before her eyes even opened.

Her body still felt like it was floating—a mix of jet lag, love, and happiness wrapped into one.

Pablo lay beside her, one arm flung across her waist, his hair a tousled mess, his breathing deep and even.

She turned onto her side and studied him, tracing the light stubble along his jaw with her eyes.

It hit her again—he was her husband.

"My husband," she whispered out loud, just to try it.

Pablo's eyes fluttered open. "Did I hear that right?" he murmured, voice raspy from sleep. "Say it again." She laughed. "My husband."

He groaned happily and pulled her in closer. "That sounds better than any goal I've ever scored."

They spent their days wrapped in bliss on the Amalfi Coast, tucked away in a private villa overlooking turquoise waves and cliffs draped in bougainvillea. No paparazzi. No training schedules. No deadlines.

Just them.

Mornings were slow and sweet. Breakfasts on the terrace, her legs draped over his as they sipped espresso and nibbled pastries. He would sneak kisses between bites, smearing powdered sugar on her cheek just to lick it off.

"Your phone's buzzing again," Pablo noted on their third morning, nodding toward her device, which was lighting up with notifications.

Bianca reached for it lazily, scrolling through. "More congratulations. Oh, and your team sent us a champagne basket... it's waiting at the front desk."

"And your mother wants to know if we're eating properly," Pablo added, reading the messages over her shoulder.

Bianca laughed and turned the phone face down. "The world can wait another week."

Pablo kissed her temple. "Or more."

Afternoons meant wandering through lemon groves, chasing each other through narrow cobblestone streets, trying to speak broken Italian to amused locals. They bought gelato three times a day and kissed on every quiet corner.

One afternoon, they got hopelessly lost in a maze of narrow alleyways. What should have been a quick trip to a local market turned into a two-hour adventure, with each turn leading them further into the heart of a village that wasn't on any tourist map.

"We should ask for directions," Bianca suggested, her

sundress fluttering in the warm breeze.

Pablo shook his head stubbornly. "I know exactly where we are."

"Really? Where?"

"Italy," he replied with a straight face before breaking into laughter at her exasperated expression.

They eventually stumbled upon a tiny restaurant tucked between ancient stone buildings. The elderly owner, seeing their flushed faces and hearing Pablo's atrocious attempt at Italian, took pity on them. She ushered them to a table in her kitchen and served them a meal that wasn't on any menu—homemade pasta tossed with fresh tomatoes and herbs from her garden.

Bianca watched, fascinated, as the woman worked, asking questions through gestures and the few Italian words she knew. By the end of the meal, they were exchanging cooking secrets like old friends, with Pablo attempting to translate and making a beautiful mess of it.

"That," Bianca declared as they finally found their way back to their villa at sunset, "was better than any five-star restaurant."

"Getting lost with you might be my new favourite hobby," Pablo replied, swinging their linked hands.

"Do we have to go back to real life?" Bianca sighed later that evening, resting her head on Pablo's shoulder as they sat on a bench overlooking the sea.

He slipped his hand into hers. "Let's just stay here forever. Open a tiny bakery. You bake, and I greet the guests in bad Italian."

She laughed. "You wouldn't last a week without football."

He grinned. "True. But I'd still try. For you."

Nights were even softer. Candlelit dinners under the stars, soft jazz playing in the distance. They talked about everything—their future, their fears, silly childhood stories they hadn't told yet. Sometimes, they just sat in silence, fingers entwined, hearts completely full.

One night, as they lay in bed, tangled in each other and the sounds of the sea, Bianca whispered, "Do you ever think we'll get tired of this? Of each other?"

Pablo propped himself on his elbow, brushing a strand of hair from her face. "Never," he said with certainty. "You're my home now."

Tears pricked at her eyes. "I never thought I'd have this. I didn't grow up dreaming of weddings or happily-ever-afters, but... this? You? It's better than anything I ever imagined."

He kissed her slowly. "We'll keep making it better. Every day."

On their last night, as they packed their suitcases with reluctance, Pablo found Bianca on the terrace, looking out at the moonlit sea.

"What are you thinking about?" he asked, wrapping his arms around her from behind.

"Real life," she said softly. "Training starts for you next week. I have three catering events lined up. Our schedules will be crazy again."

He rested his chin on her shoulder. "Are you worried?"

She turned in his arms. "No. Actually, I'm excited. I love this bubble we've been in, but I'm also ready to start our real life together. Our home. Our routines. Maybe even a family someday."

Pablo's eyes lit up. "Little football players with your cooking skills?"

"Or little chefs with your left foot," she countered, smiling.

He kissed her, slow and deep, a promise of all that was to come. "I can't wait for every minute of it."

And as they fell asleep, the windows open to the night breeze and the sound of waves. Bianca smiled to herself.

They weren't just in love.

They were in their forever.

And tomorrow, they would begin writing the next chapter together.

Epilogue: A Life of Love and New Beginnings

They built a life filled with laughter, love, and a thousand tiny moments that made up their forever. Between the buzzing streets of London where Pablo's career had reached legendary status and the sun soaked shores of Rio where they returned for extended family visits, they raised three incredible children —each one a beautiful blend of them both, carrying pieces of their heritage, their dreams, and their spirits.

Lucas, their firstborn, was now seven and already obsessed with football in a way that made Pablo both proud and nostalgic. Every surface in their home became a makeshift pitch—the hallway, the garden, even the dining room when Bianca wasn't looking. Cushions became goalposts, and more than one lamp had been sacrificed to his enthusiasm.

"Left foot, son," Pablo would call out during their garden practice sessions. "Feel the ball, don't just kick it."

Lucas would scrunch his face in concentration, tongue poking out slightly—exactly like Bianca did when perfecting a recipe—before executing a move with surprising precision for someone whose feet seemed too big for his body.

"Did you see that, Dad? Just like you against Manchester!"

Pablo would sweep him up in a hug, whispering, "Even better than me," and meaning every word. In quiet moments, he'd confide to Bianca his mix of emotions— the joy of seeing his passion live on, balanced with his determination never to pressure their son the way his own father once had.

"I want him to love it because it brings him joy, not because it might bring him glory," he'd say, and Bianca would squeeze his hand, loving him all the more for the father he had become.

Sofia, five years old with wild curls that refused any attempt at taming, was their gentle fire. She had inherited Bianca's artistic eye and Pablo's expressive nature —a combination that made her both captivating and occasionally overwhelming. One afternoon, she marched into the living room where Pablo was reviewing game footage, her tiny hands on her hips.

"Daddy, I've decided I'm going to be a chef, a princess, AND a scientist—maybe all at once." Her declaration was delivered with such conviction that Pablo didn't dare question the logistics.

"The world needs more princess-chef-scientists," he agreed solemnly, hiding his smile.

Sofia followed Bianca around the kitchen like a devoted apprentice, her special step stool positioned strategically at the counter. She insisted on wearing her tiara with her apron, creating the most enchanting contradiction.

"Mama, does this sauce need more... imagination?" she'd ask seriously, wielding a wooden spoon like a magic wand.

Bianca would pretend to consider this deeply. "I think you're right. Three drops of imagination, please."

Sofia would carefully mime adding invisible drops, her face a picture of concentration. "There! Now it will taste like sunshine."

And somehow, when Bianca tasted it afterward, it almost did.

And then there was Mateo—the wild card. Just three years old, but already the loudest voice in any room. With Pablo's athletic prowess and none of his restraint, he was constantly in motion—climbing furniture, chasing the family's patient golden retriever, or launching himself from seemingly impossible heights with complete faith that someone would catch him.

"He doesn't walk into a room; he announces himself," Bianca's mother would say during visits, equal parts exasperated and charmed.

One memorable Sunday morning, while Bianca and Pablo attempted a rare moment of peace with coffee on their terrace, they heard a crash followed by suspicious silence.

Their eyes met over their mugs.

"Your son," they said simultaneously, then dissolved into laughter before hurrying to investigate.

They found Mateo standing amid a dusting of flour, looking like a very pleased ghost.

"I making breakfast," he announced proudly. "Like Mama."

Bianca bit her lip, torn between laughter and despair at the state of her kitchen.

Pablo knelt beside their youngest. "That's very thoughtful,

my son. Maybe next time we can help you?"

Mateo considered this briefly before nodding. "OK. But I still the chef boss."

Later, as they cleaned up together, Pablo smeared a bit of flour on Bianca's cheek. "He gets that from you, you know. The 'chef boss' part."

"And the chaos is all you, football star," she retorted, flicking water his way.

Their days were messy, busy, and sometimes overwhelming—the calendar on their refrigerator was a complex algorithm of school runs, football practices, dance classes, playdates, and work commitments. But no matter how chaotic life became, they maintained sacred rituals: Sunday family dinners where phones were banned, bedtime stories that Pablo performed with different voices for each character, and date nights where they remembered they were more than just parents.

On one such night, at a small Italian restaurant tucked away from paparazzi, Pablo reached for Bianca's hand across the table. "Do you ever miss the simplicity? Before kids, before the crazy fame, when it was just us and our crazy contract?"

Bianca's eyes softened in the candlelight. "Sometimes. But I wouldn't trade this beautiful chaos for anything."

"Not even for uninterrupted sleep?" he teased.

"Well, let's not be hasty," she laughed.

Epilogue 2: The Forever After

One golden evening, ten years into their marriage, they sat on the warm sand watching their children play at the water's edge. Lucas, now a teenager with Pablo's height and Bianca's thoughtfulness, was teaching his younger siblings how to bodysurf, his patience remarkable. Sofia, artistic and dreamy, was collecting shells for an elaborate sand sculpture. Mateo, still the family tornado at eight, was racing in and out of the gentle waves, his laughter carrying on the breeze.

The sky was a masterpiece of colour—molten gold melting into deep rose and lavender. The same colours that had painted the sky on their wedding day.

Bianca leaned into Pablo's side, his arm automatically coming around her shoulders, their bodies still fitting together perfectly after all these years.

"I still can't believe this is our life," she said softly.

Pablo kissed the top of her head, breathing in the scent of coconut sunscreen and the faint trace of vanilla that always seemed to cling to her skin, no matter what she'd been cooking.

"It's better than anything I imagined," he replied, his voice deeper now, touched with the wisdom of a decade of partnership and parenthood.

They sat in comfortable silence for a moment, watching as Mateo ran up to Lucas, demanding to be thrown higher in the waves. Sofia had wandered further down the beach, collecting treasures in the folds of her skirt.

Pablo says, "Look at us now." His eyes were serious suddenly, full of a decade of memories. "You became a world-renowned chef. I became a father who can make dinosaur-shaped pancakes. We figured it out as we went along."

He took her hand, running his thumb over the simple gold band that matched his own. "That's what I love most about our story, Bianca. We never knew what was coming next, but we faced it together."

A shriek of delight pulled their attention back to the water, where Lucas had lifted Sofia onto his shoulders, her arms spread wide like she was flying.

"They're growing up so fast," Bianca murmured, a hint of melancholy in her voice.

"That's how it works, my love," Pablo replied gently. "But think of all we still have ahead. Lucas's first real football match. Sofia's art exhibitions—you know she's going to be famous one day. Mateo's... well, whatever tornado path he chooses."

Bianca laughed. "College graduations. Maybe weddings someday. Grandchildren."

"Gray hair," Pablo added, tugging playfully at a silver strand escaping from her ponytail.

"Speak for yourself," she retorted, poking his ribs where a slight softness had replaced the footballer's hard muscle. His playing days were behind him now—a coaching position was keeping him in the game he loved without the physical toll.

He caught her hand, bringing it to his lips. "You know what else we have to look forward to?" "What?"

"More nights like this. More sunsets. More moments when I look at you and think I'm the luckiest man alive."

Tears pricked at Bianca's eyes. "How do you still make me cry with your words after all this time?"

"It's my superpower," he said with a wink. "That, and my legendary left foot."

Their laughter mingled with the sound of the waves, a harmony they had perfected over years.

As the sun dipped below the horizon, painting the sky in impossible colours, their children's laughter echoed along the shore. Lucas was now helping Sofia with her sand sculpture while Mateo ran circles around them, narrating an elaborate story only he understood.

Pablo stood, offering his hand to Bianca. "Dance with me?"

"Here? Now? There's no music," she protested, even as she placed her hand in his.

"There's always music with you," he said simply, pulling her to her feet and into his arms.

They swayed together at the edge of the ocean, barefoot in the wet sand, as the first stars appeared above them. No choreography, no audience—just two people still in love with the story they were writing together.

The children noticed after a moment, exchanging glances before abandoning their activities to join them. Lucas dramatically dipped Sofia, who giggled uncontrollably.

111

Mateo inserted himself between his parents, demanding to be included.

Soon, they were all dancing, a family constellation moving together under the vast sky, creating a moment that would live in all their memories.

Because some stories don't end with "happily ever after."

They continue evolving, growing richer and deeper with each passing year.

Some love stories—the best ones—just keep getting better.

THE END

Acknowledgement

Writing a book is like preparing an elaborate feast—impossible without passion, determination, and stolen moments between life's many demands. As I close this chapter of Bianca and Pablo's story, I'm filled with gratitude for those who were part of this journey.

To my darling husband—thank you for being part of this journey and for your patience when talking to me and realising I was in another world.

To my beautiful children—thank you for understanding when Mommy needed "just five more minutes" (that turned into hours), for your enthusiastic hugs when I finally emerged from my writing cave, and for inspiring me with your limitless imagination. The joy you bring to my life flavours every word I write.

To my wonderful mum, who first sparked my love for the kitchen and introduced me to the magic of books—your wisdom and warmth have shaped not only my stories but who I am.

And to my incredible dad, whose boundless creativity and artistic spirit flow through my veins—thank you for showing me that imagination has no limits. The two of you gave me the greatest gifts: roots and wings.

To my beloved grandmother, who planted the seeds of my passion for football by welcoming me beside her to watch every match on her television since I was just a little kid. Those countless hours of shared excitement, disappointment, and triumph not only fostered my love for the beautiful game but also taught me about dedication, persistence, and the pure joy of being swept up in something greater than yourself. The spirit of Pablo's love for football was born in your living room.

The stories we create are never truly our own—they're a tapestry woven from the threads of everyone who has touched our lives. Thank you all for being part of mine.

To my friends who read early drafts—your honest feedback and unwavering support carried me through moments of doubt and celebration alike.

This book was truly a labour of love—written in early mornings before the house stirred, during school hours, and late into the night after dishes were done and lunches packed for the next day. Every word was crafted, edited, and polished by my own hand, between the countless responsibilities of motherhood and running a household. There were moments when it seemed impossible, but the story insisted on being told.

To everyone who cheered me on (or listened to me ramble about fictional people like they were real)—thank you. Your encouragement made this book possible. And to the dreamers, readers, and hopeless romantics—this one's for you.

Lastly, to you, dear reader, for choosing to spend time in the world I've created—there is no greater honour than sharing this story with you. I hope it leaves you hungry for love, adventure, and maybe a good Brazilian feijoada.

With gratitude and love,

B. Oneirova

About The Author

B. Oneirova

From the Greek "oneiros," meaning "dream" is a romance author who believes in the power of happy endings—not just in books, but in life. Though she can't make that a reality for everyone, she channels this wish into stories that bring others the same joy and comfort that happy stories have given her.

A lifelong storyteller (and admittedly, a great talker), B. finds in writing her true voice. Her stories, including elements of "A Recipe for Love," often begin as dreams and have been her escape, joy, and way of making sense of the world.

After keeping her writing private for years, B. finally realized that stories—like good meals—are meant to be shared. This debut novel represents her first step into sharing the worlds she's built in her imagination.

When not writing, B. can be found experimenting in the kitchen (much like Bianca), getting lost in other people's books, and searching for those small, perfect moments that make life beautiful.

"I hope this story feels like a warm hug in your soul in a world that sometimes forgets the magic of happy endings."

Connect With Me

Dear Reader,

Thank you for joining Bianca and Pablo on their journey from strangers to soulmates. Their story has been a joy to share, and I hope it brought you as much happiness reading it as it brought me while writing it.

I'd love to hear what you thought of "A Recipe for Love"! Your review on Amazon, Kindle or Goodreads helps other readers discover this story and means the world to me. Even just a sentence or two makes a tremendous difference to a new author.

Stay in Touch!

Email: dreamweavertales80@gmail.com

Instagram: @dreamweavertales

TikTok: @dreamweavertales80

Facebook: @DreamweaverTales

Coming Soon

I'm currently working on a brand new book featuring two new characters named Bethany and Jack. Their story will take you on an unexpected journey filled with challenges, connection, and courage. Stay tuned for more details...

With heartfelt gratitude,

B. Oneirova

Printed in Dunstable, United Kingdom